With Feeling Plus Stuff

Kate Breuer

Published by Kate Breuer, 2024.

This is a work of fiction. Similarities to real people, places, or events are entirely coincidental.

WITH FEELING PLUS STUFF

First edition. September 22, 2024.

Copyright © 2024 Kate Breuer.

ISBN: 979-8227345608

Written by Kate Breuer.

Also by Kate Breuer

Water & Earth
Spores

Standalone
Out of Hiding
Chase: The Trilogy
With Feeling Plus Stuff

Watch for more at https://katehildenbrand.com/.

I found myself while writing this book. This book is for anyone who hasn't found themselves. Keep looking.

Pandora's box

The apartment is quiet, cool, and calm when Nik tip-toes through the hall. He balances his bowl in one hand, the dog's food in the other, his *Kindle* stuffed haphazardly underneath an arm, as he sidesteps the trash that is stacked three bins high next to the front door.

"You know the drill, Marv," he whispers with half a glance toward the door behind which Percy is snoring. Audibly. Fuck, how can such a tiny person be so loud? "Go to your place."

He almost drops his stupid reader trying to set the food bowl down before he rearranges the items in his hands. He sits down with his own breakfast, wondering if this is going to be another 12-steps-to-make-tea kinda day.

Marvin whines from her bed. "I haven't forgotten about you, little shit." He knows he should ignore the dog. *Attention as a reward for begging. Great job, Nikau.*

He leans the reader against the fruit bowl and digs into the oatmeal.

"Oh, for fuck's sake, dog. Shut it!" he snaps when Marvin gives another low whine. It's the kind of whine that escapes. Marvin is trying. And Nik is fucking yelling at her. He has half a mind to get up and apologize to his dog when a voice from the other end of the hall makes Marvin forget about not just the snapping but Nik's very existence. "Free," Nik's wife commands.

"I wasn't done eating," he states by way of morning greeting. So much for teaching the dog anything. She walks by to press a kiss onto his cheek, before vanishing into the bathroom with a mumbled "Sorry."

Nik rubs a hand down his face and makes himself take a deep breath. Did she take her phone? Nik has long since wondered if he should consider her visits to the bathroom *Reddit* holes instead. But, he's not complaining. With both of them working from home, any moment alone is cherished.

He is three sentences away from finishing his chapter, when she reemerges with an annoyed wail.

Just as suddenly, Henry releases him roughly enough that he staggers backward, and—[1]

Another wail, more pronounced. 'What happened?" he asks as he shuts down the *Kindle*.

"I have to present this new proposal in an hour, and Ralph still hasn't gotten me the numbers I need for the final slides. I asked him for them six weeks ago. And now it's Saturday and he's not working.

She sits down opposite him, and flops her phone down on the table. He fights the urge to check her unprotected phone for scratches, and sits on his hands instead.

"Have you tried calling him?" He tries, and her deep sigh tells him, she doesn't want a solution, so he shuts up and listens instead.

He tries to follow as she walks him through the proposal, what feels like every related policy ever written into law, and the calculations behind whatever Ralph is supposed to send her.

"Sounds reasonable," is all he can offer, when she raises and expectant eyebrow over a cup of coffee she must have made while talking.

"See," she snaps. "*You* get it. It's not that hard."

Considering that everything she does is so far above his head he can't even see the top of the wall he is trying to vault, he is impressed he has been able to follow at all. He knows the people at Bold Industries are probably all smarter than him. Being used as the bar for stupidity somehow doesn't feel less degrading if the bar is applied to smart people.

He opens his mouth, closes it, takes his bowl to the sink, and opens the tap. "Is there anything I can help you with?" he asks her while he washes the slimy remains of his oatmeal from the pottery.

"Not really," she answers, and he knows she is going through a list of tasks too complicated to even explain to him. He knows he can't help, but he can't think of any other way to show his support.

Without another word, she sets her mug down on the counter next to the sink, and walks toward the study. He huffs and picks up the mug with his gloved hand.

Costa Rica, here I come, he thinks to himself. Nik has never been to Costa Rica. His Spanish is more than rusty. He doesn't even think his uneducated ass would get a visa. But a guy can dream, and Costa Rica is his escape. He's not even sure when it took up the place in his mind. Sure, there had been that one dude in school he'd been friends with. They'd lost touch later when he packed up a year before graduation and moved to Costa Rica with nothing more than a backpack. For all he knew, his friend had failed and gone home.

But Nik has the whole Schrödinger thing down to a T. As long as he doesn't find out otherwise, Fabian is pursuing his life's dreams and adventures in Costa Rica.

This Schrödinger dude really was a genius.

He has cleaned and dried all the dishes, wiped down the surfaces, and even brought down the trash, when Percy swirls around him again. She talks about the proposal—again!—and he feels himself drifting away from the conversation.

"Thank you for listening." Percy drags him from his daydreams of a land he doesn't yet know, and he begins to rewind the conversation in his head. He stares at her, caught by the three lines between her eyebrows: two to the right, one to the left.

"I know what you were talking about," he starts. Something about her father, the board maybe? Ah, *that* rant.

"Cheeks, really," he urges, the use of the pet name intentional. If he catches her mood early, he can prevent a day wasted on arguments. "Those bastards on the board don't value you enough. Maybe you should remind them who's at the top of your dad's will."

Percy scoffs, and he knows she's impressed against her will that he has bullshitted his way out of this one—again. "Unless you are offering to get rid of my father for me—and I'm not saying I would object—it doesn't matter what his will says. You know my father: He will probably run the stupid company from his death bed."

"You think death will keep him away from that ugly black leather chair?" Nik chuckles at the idea of Percy's father pulling a *Binns*. "He will die, and his ghost will get up and go to work."

She doesn't get the reference, because she has never shared his *Harry Potter* obsession.

"Marvin needs a walk," he announces and is half-way to the leash on a hook by the door, when he realizes Percy might not have been done talking. He looks up at her while kneeling next to a very excited Marvin. "I'm sorry. I can stay."

She shakes her head. "No, it's fine. Go. There's nothing you can do."

The world fades away as the headphones seal over his ears. He fumbles with his phone, as Marvin jumps down the stairs, dragging him along.

"*I am not throwing away my shot. I'm just like my country. I am young, scrappy and hungry, and I am not throwing away my shot,*" Lin-Manuel Miranda sings in his ear moments later, pushing more of the sounds around him away until he hears nothing but the upbeat melody of his favorite musical.

He is determined to get himself out of this rut. His bare feet carry him to the nearby forest, the damp grass fresh around his toes. Bird song manages to drill through the music in his ears. He lets Marvin off the leash and doesn't try to stop the grin building on his face as autumn leaves, a sunset of red, orange, and yellow, are sent flying by energy penned up in sixty pounds of fluff.

There are three loops through the forest, but even the largest one won't do today. He wishes he could close the fucking Pandora's box that opened over the past months. Why can't he just stuff all his shitty feelings and realizations back into the box, close it, lock it, stuff it into the furthest corner of their over-sized attic, and never look at them again?

Life was easier with a mask on his face, but—boy—was he itching to take it off. Things had been a lot less complicated when he had thought he loved his wife.

I mean, to be fair, it was still true. Kinda. In a way. The problem, the fucking problem, was that he wasn't *in love* with his wife. Shit, way too much of the time, he wasn't even sure he still *liked* his wife.

Stop it!

He forces the smile back onto his face. *Fake it 'till you make it,* or something. Whatever. He is determined to stay in good spirits—or get there. Who cares?

Marvin supplies the much-needed distraction when she pelts toward Nik, almost knocking him over despite his sturdy build. Nik laughs loudly and with a mumbled, "Ah, fuck it," joins Marvin in the leaves. They play, wrestle, and roll around for what feels like hours but is probably more like ten minutes. They only stop when Marv loses interest, and starts licking her front paws with elegant languidness instead.

"I love you, you stupid, stupid dog!" Nik digs his face into the fur at Marvin's neck before getting up and rifling through the leaves for the leash. He claps a palm to his thigh. "Come on."

With a shrug, he fishes his phone out of his pocket and texts his wife:

Marvin still isn't tired out after the largest round. Good luck with your meeting.

A proud parade

Slimy paint hits his cheeks and he squeals. "Fuck's this, Dee?"

"You need some more color on your face, honey!"

He holds still, lets her finish patiently, before pushing her hand away. "Stop fussing."

"But she does it so well," his mom answers, as she dips her own finger into the paint and—hold on—eats it? "This is delicious, sweetie."

Dee's lip twitches when she holds the tin out to Vasco. "Edible face paint. Isn't it just absolutely *brilliant?*"

He holds the paint to his nose, and a fruity sweetness hits him. There's a hint of something else that makes him think vanilla, but he can't think of a reason to add vanilla to face paint.

"New project?" he asks Dee who is busy applying color to her mother's face.

Dee's dramatic shrug makes her dress's shoulder pads lift. "I don't know. It's not that easy. It's an idea I've been toying with. The texture is still all wrong, though. And then there's all this regulation. Labeling it as edible means meeting food standards in addition to makeup standards. And, ah, I don't know. It's a lot to think about. But with all the ingredients in conventional face paint… I don't know. It's an idea."

She says all of this very fast, and Vasco pulls her into a hug that lifts her off her feet. Well, and almost knocks the tray out of her hands.

"What did I do?" she asks, but hugs him back with equal enthusiasm. "I've missed you, too, Vassy." She wiggles him from side to side, before letting him go. "I've missed you, too."

His youngest sister Jo bounces off the wall she's been sitting on and waves her phone at them. "Your wife's running late, Mom."

He reads the message on the screen: **Running late. ETA: 7 min.**

"Aren't you glad to have your own place?" Jo asks him.

"Oh, the peace and quiet!" he admits. He doesn't mention *Mount Dishmore* next to his sink. Jo shoves him a little, and they wrestle—more like she wrestles and he lets her—for a moment until Dee pulls them apart.

The crowd grows around them, as they wander around to find a good spot. They decide on a small pedestrian bridge that crosses the parade route.

"I'm here. I'm here." His mama is half-running toward them, his middle two sisters struggling to keep up behind her, while she knots the light blue, pink, and white of the transgender flag into her high bun.

"The crowds are insane!" Ella explains with a wave around.

His mama scowls at her. "Ella, language."

His mama looks ready to release a rant Vasco knows by heart, but before Vasco can finish the thought, Giàu comes to the rescue. "Picture time," his youngest sister announces. Giàu can always be relied on to avoid confrontation of any kind. Gigi has a very special version of shyness Vasco learned to predict over the years of reading her bedtime stories and helping with her homework.

Ella wrangles the family into a friendly arrangement, before handing her phone to a pink-sequined stranger, and slipping between him and Jo. They smile for a photo, take a few more with goofy grins, rabbit ears, and peace signs. Vasco's phone buzzes before pink-sequin guy has finished saying good-bye.

Vasco taps the notification. His family's stock-photo-for-diversity look is amped up by the rainbow flags and his mama's transgender scarf. "We look ridiculous," he judges, and saves the photo to his favorites.

Picture duty fulfilled, Jo and Dee pull him toward a nearby booth selling ice cream and cotton candy. His sisters get a bit of everything while he's too fascinated by the sign explaining how the heat produced while cooling the ice cream is used to produce the cotton candy. Impressive. They pull him away to share the sweet treats in the grass next to the booth.

"You want to join in?" His mom asks, already on her feet to run down the hill. The laughing crowd below has started to dance. Vasco lets his sisters tug him back to his feet. He helps up Jo, and they run down the hill, Jo's arms wide in the air, her whoop tearing on his eardrums.

They dance, sing, chant with the crowd. He lets Jo climb onto his back when she can't stand any longer, and soon after sets her down on the lawn. They dance around her—Jo's upper-body dance no less enthusiastic—until their feet hurt and their sweat has mixed with that of the hundreds around them.

Exhausted and with ringing ears, Vasco collapses onto the grass. He stares at the clouds, humming along with the tireless crowd. His eyes are threatening to shutter when something cold touches his cheeks, and he is wide awake again.

A glimpse of huge blue eyes is the only warning before the dog's tongue is in his face, licking off every bit of the paint Dee applied.

"Marvin, no." The dog, runs toward the call, and Vasco turns to see what he suspects to be some kind of Australian Shepherd mutt run toward a figure in the distance.

"Sorry about that," the silhouette calls. Vasco waves him off with a smile and a "No problem, man."

When his family spreads out around him, he leans back on his elbows. Ella, Jo, and his mama pass out paper plates with burritos. The conversation around Vasco ebbs in and out of focus as he enjoys his food, salsa dripping from the corner of his mouth onto the grass. His mom leaves and returns with beers and sodas, and with a deep draught of Sierra Nevada, Vasco resigns himself to the fact that he won't get any school work done tonight either.

He inspects each of the people around him in turn, weighing his choices. Decision made, he leans over to Gigi and whispers, "Please keep my hangover to a minimum, Gi."

The choice bears some risks, but success is guaranteed. Giàu makes up with reliability, resourcefulness, and a thorough lack of shame, what she lacks in volume. And there is no telling which family member she might involve to keep her promise.

"I'll watch over you," Gigi whispers back, as she squeezes his knee with her small hand. She winks at him, before scooting closer to Jo to share in Jo's nachos.

Everything is fucked

Nik's fingers fly over the keyboard, as he types. An email, the script for his next podcast episode, a blog post: words fly out of his brain this morning. With a sense of accomplishment, he pulls up the essay he has been working on for weeks:

Gender-tainted Expressions in a Gender-neutral Language.

I need a better title. He selects the title with his mouse. A few letters typed, deleted, typed, deleted, the screen now reads:

How Do We Manage to Fuck up Gender-neutrality in a Non-gendered Language like English?

"Fuck," he growls, and Marvin opens an eye on the giant gray pet bed next to where Nik sits leaned against the wall. "I bet dogs don't have to think about all of this shit, do they?"

Marvin's right ear pokes up and her gentle blue eyes focus on Nik. Nik leans over to scratch her between the ears, before he forces his attention back to his laptop. A few rounds of command-Z return the title to the previous state as he scans what he has written so far.

The paragraphs have been written, rewritten, edited, and polished. Even Nik can't find anything to correct. But, he also can't figure out how to finish the damned thing. It's missing something and he has no clue what.

Without adding or altering a single word, he closes the essay and pulls up his journal instead.

He takes a deep breath, eyes closed, expels the air, and begins to type. There is so much in his head to get out, to sort through, to understand. Yet, after half an hour of starting, stopping, deleting, and rewriting, the screen only holds three words:

Everything is fucked.

Shaking his head at his own eloquence, he sets aside his laptop. His head hits the wall when he leans back on his cushion, stretches his leg over the hardwood under the floor desk. *Amazing how quickly one can go from accomplished motivation to desperation and a general feeling of fucked-ness.*

He abandons his laptop, desk, and any hope of getting more work done. When he gets up, Marvin's head lifts hopefully, and the blue stare follows him across the room as he grabs the *Kindle* from the shelf and sits down in his reading chair—the only spot in his room normal people would consider comfortable.

His shitty mood lifts slowly, as he makes it through page after page of his current read. It's a fluffy romance that is nothing like the books he usually reads. He can't even remember how it made its way onto his reading list.

He jumps when his door opens and immediately shuts the book. Before she has fully poked her head through the door, he has pulled up his latest nonfiction read instead.

He is absolutely not going to let her see him reading romance novels. *One* romance novel, he corrects himself. *Four romance novels do not a reading habit make.*

"Hiding something?" his wife asks, as she opens the door a bit wider.

He shakes his head. "I was just..."

Percy waves him off, the smile falling off her face. "I'm waiting for something to finish uploading, so I'll have lunch a little early."

She walks back out of his room without closing his door. Marvin jumps up to follow her.

Nik runs a hand over his dreads, shuts down the reader and places it on the little stool next to his reading chair. With that, he gives up on reading and writing, and follows Marvin and Percy into the kitchen. *Like an obedient little puppy.*

When he enters the kitchen, Percy is busy making herself lunch. "Do you want to eat anything?" She asks when she sees him.

Nik opens the fridge and scans the contents. The fridge isn't empty but it feels like there is nothing in there. "I don't know."

"Can you check on my bread rolls?" she asks, but doesn't wait for a response before walking out of the kitchen.

Nik peers into the oven where the bread rolls are still pale, before refocusing on his own lunch. Without feeling like eating anything, he grabs a container from the fridge and heats a pan. Leftover pasta with veggies it is.

The bread rolls are cooling on a rack on the counter when Percy finally reemerges. Without comment, she grabs the rolls and starts assembling her sandwiches, while Nik struggles to find time for his own meal preparations.

He stirs his pasta, grabs water from the fridge, finds a suitable plate, and is in the process of heaping food onto it, when he hears his wife sit down. "My food is getting cold," she states, and he can't suppress the eye roll. *Well, maybe if he didn't have to use divination to guess when we have lunch, figure out what to eat, and watch your food while I prep mine, I would be done at the same time.*

"I'll be right there," he says instead. "Feel free to start without me."

He grabs the handful of pills from the counter and shoves them into his mouth. Rushing to ensure the right amount of time between swallowing the damned pills–too early and he'll ruin his appetite, too late, and he'll get nauseous–he sits down from Percy.

She is halfway through her food when he stabs the first noodle. She doesn't talk during lunch, but instead stares at her phone. She looks busy, so he shuts up.

A few minutes later, he is finishing his food, and trying very hard not to throw the plate she has left on the table after her. "Could you put your plate next to the sink, at least?" He asks with as little reproach as he can manage. *Why can't you just do that without me asking you to?*

She twirls around, grabs the plate, and deposits it next to the sink where it sits precariously on top of a cutting board and three other plates. He shakes his head the tiniest amount and abandons the rest of his pasta.

His stomach is already complaining, and he knows it's not good to eat more. *And now I need a break from this fucked-up lunch break.*

When he walks past Percy's room to go back to his own for a nap, her door is open. Percy is under the sheets on her bed, eyes closed, face relaxed.

Nik hesitates, eying his own door with longing, thinking of the short nap and the productive afternoon he had planned out to get everything done before the fucking fundraiser tonight.

He's still hovering in the hallway when Percy opens her eyes and smiles a rare smile. "Join me?" she asks and holds open her arms.

With a mental *Fuck it* Nik discards his shirt and pants on the reading chair and climbs into her bed. She waits for him to cuddle up at her side, his head resting on her chest, his arms around her hip, before lowering her own arms around him. Nik finds himself relaxing into the affection, feels his eyes flutter closed, and his mind shut off.

I can make that work

She is warm against his back when he wakes, her arm around his waist, fingers tracing the lines of his abdominal muscles. Even with the haze dragging him back to sleep, something tells him she hasn't slept even for a second.

When her fingers suddenly stop their repetitive motion on his chest—He hadn't even noticed how much it had bothered him.—he turns to face her. Her eyes find his. "Hey." Sleep roughens his whisper. "Are you okay?"

"Fine," she answers too quickly. "Just work shit."

He rolls over completely, and pulls her into his arms. Her body finds its spot like two pieces of a whole sliding together. She breathes him in, kisses the spot where his shoulder meets his neck, just above the collarbone.

His palm is circling her back in what he hopes is a comforting fashion. "Work is killing you, Cheeks."

She digs her face into his neck, and he pulls her closer. He's here for her. The words "I love you" hang on his lips, but he catches them before they escape. It might technically be true, but it still feels like a lie, and Nik has promised himself to never lie again.

"I know what would help," Percy says, and he knows there is a mischievous grin on the lips that kiss his neck.

"Oh, yeah?" he grins back.

She slides her hand into his boxer, and breathes a quiet "Yeah" onto his skin.

They fool around, fingers and mouths exploring each other's bodies until Percy's phone rings them both out of their escape. "Ten minutes," she breathes, while thumbing the snooze button. He watches her mind drift back to reality behind her eyes and shrugs a shoulder. "I can make that work."

Before she can tell him there isn't enough time, before she can even overthink, he kisses a trail down her body. He slows enough to give her a chance to choose reality, but then his mouth is between her legs to finish a job he started an hour ago.

Ten minutes later, sweat clings to both of they bodies. Percy's eyes are closed, and he watches the rise and fall of her chest slow. When her eyes find his, he sees panic flush away the orgasm-induced endorphins.

"Fuck," she groans. "I'll be late."

She jumps up, barely catching his gaze, before grabbing clothes from the floor, and dressing in record speed. "Sorry," she mumbles on the way out. She is almost out of sight, when she turns around, plants a giant kiss on his forehead, then half-jogs toward the bathroom.

The sweat feels sticky and cold on Nik's skin without her warmth. He leans back into the pillows, closes his eyes for a moment, and forces himself out of her bed. Where are his fucking boxers? He digs through the pile on the floor. He is elbow-deep in the mess of blankets and sheets on her bed, when he hears the toilet flush. *Fuck it.*

"Marv, come on." With a yawn and a downward dog that would make Nik's former yoga instructor proud, Marvin gets up and slow-motion-walks across the hall. He slumps down in the pet bed next to Nik's desk and the soothing blue eyes close before Nik has even shut the door.

He hears her pass outside, wants to feel her in his arms again, wants to feel like he belongs, but she is late for her meeting and... it doesn't matter. He has work to do, and a two-hour lunch break—even on a Sunday—isn't exactly conductive to a checked-off to-do list.

Fluffy rainbow-glitter slippers

Gigi has kept her promise—though he cannot for the life of him remember how. His memory of the previous night is fuzzy. Flashes of rainbow colors, his family dancing, Jo's head against his neck when he carried her to the car. And beer, definitely beer.

"Do you need help with your bow tie?"

The Ella he finds in his doorway looks nothing like his little sister. Granted, she hasn't been little in a while, but with her hair tamed into an elegant bun, and her lips the shade of squashed blackberries, she looks... older. And her dress? Damn if that's not going to turn a few teenage heads tonight.

"You look great!"

And she does, but he'll always prefer the thick waves of hazelnut he used to braid for her when she was younger.

She looks him up and down, her eyes scrutinizing every inch from his unkempt hair to the pink, fluffy rainbow-glitter slippers he *definitely* hasn't stolen from his mama. He would give them back, after all.

"More over-partied teenage idiot than black-tie smarts," Ella declares after what feels like eternity. "Want some help?"

Without waiting for a response, she holds out a hand to help him out of the way-too-cozy bean bag he's been working on for the past few hours.

"Thanks, Oaky!"

Ella rolls her eyes. "I'm glad Gi convinced you to spend the night. You'd be so late without us."

"I wouldn't even *attend* without you," he corrects, but as Vasco isn't even sure what time it is—very late afternoon from the light shining through the small window in his childhood room—he has to admit she has a point.

As if summoned by sisterly intuition, Dee appears in the door, satin blue swirling above heels she could kill someone with. "You ready, Vas?"

Before he can respond, she eyes him, exchanges a glance with their sister, and crosses her arms. For someone who looks absolutely nothing like their mama, she has her judgmental stare down perfectly.

"I don't even know why I have to go to this thing," he begins to argue, but Dee shoves him bodily in the direction of the door. "Shower, before you make us all late."

Vasco raises his palms and heads for the bathroom. He pushes the door closed with his foot while connecting his phone to the speaker and selecting his soundtrack.

With the secret superpower of salsa—and Ella's ability to knot a bowtie—he slides into the backseat with about thirty seconds to spare.

"Ready!" he announces with a wide grin. "Told ya!"

He can feel the eye rolls Dee and Ella exchange over the car's roof before sitting down on either side of him.

"Seriously," he adds in a low voice. "I don't know how I manage without you."

Ella leans a head onto his shoulder. "It is a miracle."

They leave on time but have to park around the block anyway. Dee and Ella hook an elbow into each of his and he pretends he doesn't notice them wobbling slightly in their heels.

Their mother walks next to them, catching secret glances at them every few meters as if they are going to prom.

"We know we look stunning, mama," Dee deadpans. "Stop staring at us."

"Can't I be proud of my little hatchlings?" She walks a few steps faster to grab a photo of them. They slow down enough to give her a chance and smile at the camera like the good children they are.

They turn the corner to find the rest of the family waiting for them. Gi wears a concrete-gray knee-length dress that reflects the light in all colors of the rainbow. It's not glitter but more of an understated shine. It's perfect for his sister.

Jo is in her wheelchair today, looking no less stunning in a short pink dress and yellow heels.

"Fuck, y'all look so good," he exclaims.

His mama's and Gi's "Language!" in predictable synchrony makes the family laugh.

"But you do," he insists when they calm down a bit. "Mama, we need another photo."

They enroll another poor passerby to take a family photo—immediately shared in the family group chat—before they head into the building.

"It's so fancy," Jo squeals when they enter an entrance hall that he can only describe as grand. Two staircases spiral on either side and meet at an open door on the upper floor where two men in white suits hand out champagne in delicate flutes.

Ella has conjured up an attendant within seconds to show them to the elevator and they vanish around a corner. Vasco climbs the stairs with the rest of his family feeling like a fucking prince or something and gladly accepts his drink at the top.

"Fucking fancy," he agrees with Jo when she and Ella reappear next to them.

His mothers excuse themselves to talk to some supposedly important people, so Vasco and his sisters set out to find their reserved table. He's glad to see his mama has listened to him and placed them toward a corner near the bar where they can enjoy themselves a bit out of the spotlight.

He has replaced his champagne with a beer when his mothers climb the stairs onto the stage. Two people he doesn't know mirror them on the other side until they stand side-by-side behind a podium. His mom steps forward and introduces first herself and her wife, then the head of some oil company and his daughter. *Really? He looks so much older than her.*

"At least she's not his wife," he whispers into Dee's ear who slaps him on the shoulder.

He doesn't listen when his mothers hold another variation of a speech he could recite in his sleep. Instead, he looks around the room, takes in the colors the many dresses and a few bolder suits sprinkle between the sea of black, and gray, and boring.

As soon as their mothers leave the stage, he downs the rest of his beer in one go and waves over a waiter. His job tonight is to look like a picture-perfect adoptive son. No reason not to make it a little more bearable.

"Whiskey. Neat."

Breasts can be so useful

Nik leans over the bar and tries to catch the eye of the barkeeper. Unfortunately, his lack of objectifiable cleavage makes it near impossible to get the man's attention.

Another body in a gray dress slides in next to him, an arm raised, and it takes an estimated 2.4 seconds for the barkeeper to appear. "Two Rosé and whatever this poor soul is having."

It takes Nik a second and a gentle poke in the side to react. "Wild Turkey 101. On the rocks, please."

The barkeeper smiles at her, then glowers at him, as if he was stealing his chance to get into the young woman's pants. Nik isn't even sure she's off age, and pretty sure the barkeeper should be checking.

"Breasts can be so useful," he says, then mentally hits himself over the head. "Sorry, I just meant that I'd been trying to get that dude's attention for a solid ten minutes."

She chuckles. "I had a lot of fun watching you struggle."

Nik stares at her mischievous smile for a moment, before he finds his manners. "Thank you. In return, let me pay for those drinks. The least I can do."

Her smile changes to something between polite and reserved, so he adds, "A purely platonic gesture, I promise."

Her eyes sparkle and the mischief returns to the smile. "In that case, let me know if my breasts can be of any more help getting horny men to look at you. Thanks!"

The barkeeper's expression shifts slightly, but Nik sees him stuff the emotion behind a flirty smile. She grabs the wine glasses, and leaves Nik to deal with the barkeeper who is holding out a hand for Nik's card. *Ah, now you are interested in me, you little shit.*

"You can put that onto my wife's tap: Persephone Miller-Simmons."

He smirks when the barkeeper's face falls. *Yep, you've been ignoring the husband of your fucking boss's boss's boss or something.*

"Of course, sir. Would you like anything else, sir?"

Nik is still grinning when he turns without another word, and walks away. He has never used his wife's position to get anything for himself but this had been worth it. Serves the dude right for lusting after teenagers and serving boobs instead of people.

He finds his wife and realizes too late who she's talking to. "Hello Mr. Miller," he says in his politest tone. He's been married to the man's daughter for 8 years, and he still doesn't get to call his father-in-law by his first name. Mr. *fucking* Miller.

"Hello Nikau." He drags the "au" out long in a way that makes it sound Chinese. Nik doesn't correct it. He never has.

"My father was just telling me his plans for the next year," Percy catches him up. "He wants to expand the drilling further into the Arctic circle."

Nik clenches his drink and forces the tone out of his voice. "I'm sure it will be prosperous for the family fortune."

"Nik," Percy hisses and bumps his side.

"No, no, Persephone. Your *husband* is quite right." He spits the word out as if it hurts his tongue to admit Nik is part of his family. "It will add a significant amount to our *company's* bank accounts, making it possible for us to fund little events like this one." He waves a hand at the ballroom. "Excuse me."

He pushes Nik aside to step through and leaves him with his wife who he is now realizing looks furious. "What did I do?" He asks before she can speak.

Her cheeks are flushed, and her jaw tense. "Why can't you just be nice to him and make my life a little less complicated?"

Because your father is a selfish egomaniac who cares about nothing but money.

"I'm really trying, Perce. But drilling the Arctic? Really?"

She grunts in frustration. "You know I don't want that either. But what am I supposed to do?"

"Quit!" he suggests before he can bite his tongue.

"I can't fix the world. Not everyone has the luxury to be an idealistic dreamer like you."

He doesn't know why the words hit him like a punch, but they do. Like a gut-wrenching fist to the guts. He shakes his head, and forces himself to walk past her. If he stays, he will say things he cannot take back. If he stays, he can't be sure what he'll do. So, he leaves. He leaves her standing in the middle of a fucking fundraiser because he doesn't know how to talk to his wife. He leaves like the coward he keeps telling himself he is.

He downs his whiskey, smashes the glass onto a nearby table with too much force, and heads for the door.

The air outside is fresh to his skin, and he gulps in cold breaths. There isn't enough air. He can't get enough air into his lungs. Knowing that he is on the verge of a panic attack does nothing to relieve the choking pressure around his chest. He can't. Fucking. Breathe.

He sinks onto the ground and squats with his hands around his head. In his gollum pose, he shuts out the world, and focuses on his breathing. *In. Out. In. Out.* When the night air doesn't feel a million tons heavy anymore, he slowly stands.

A hand steadies him when he sways on the spot. "You okay?" a gentle voice asks from behind.

When a guy in a midnight-blue suit and a shockingly pink bowtie steps into his line of sight, his look carries even more worry than his voice did.

"I'll be fine," Nik manages in a shaky voice.

The guy leads him to a bench nearby, and guides him onto the seat. "How about we sit a minute. The stars are nice tonight. It will give you a chance to catch your breath without admitting that you need to."

There is no judgement in the man's voice, no trace of superiority in the smile.

Nik chuckles weakly. "I need to."

Thick brows rise above honey-colored eyes. "Surprising."

"Surprising?" Nik asks.

"You don't look like a man who'd admit weakness."

Nik doesn't succeed in keeping his voice neutral. "You don't know me."

"Let's change that," the man says as he extends a hand. "I'm Vasco."

Vasco's voice changes when he speaks his own name, traces of Spanish that didn't reach his English.

"Look, man. I'm not really the best company right now. No offense."

The man, Vasco, smiles with a comfort and confidence Nik couldn't pull off himself. "None taken." He leans against the bench, both arms over the back and crosses one leg over the other in a figure-four. "The stars are nice tonight," he says again.

Nik can't help but laugh. The honey gaze remains intent on the clear sky above, and Nik's curiosity wins. "If I tell you my name, will you tell me why you are out here with me instead of attending the exciting happenings in there?"

Vasco turns, and his grin widens even more. "I was out here to get some fresh air. I didn't go back in because of you. First, it looked like you might need help. Then it sounded like you might need company. But you also sound like you need space to think."

"Wow," is all Nik can manage to say—or think for that matter. *Just. Fucking. Wow.* He could not have summarized his own needs better if he tried, assuming he'd gotten far enough to admit he had needs.

Vasco leans back and returns his attention to the sky. "I can see *Ursa Major* up there."

What?

Nik stares at his companion. The man's hair is tucked behind one ear, exposing a round face and a fluffy attempt at a beard. "Are you seriously talking about the constellations now?"

"Constellation. No -s. I can only name the one. And considering it's *Ursa major*, it's probably not very impressive, either."

Nik splutters for a moment, before he manages to sort his thoughts enough to form a somewhat cohesive response. "Color me impressed. I don't even know this Ursula thingy." He extends his own hand. "I'm Nik."

Duty calls

The stars glitter above and the cool night makes Vasco feel alive in a way that no party ever could. He digs around his pockets and finds a metal tube and lighter.

Next to him, Nik is looking more like the man Vasco made fun of with Gigi earlier and less like a corpse with dreadlocks.

"You smoke?" he asks and holds up the metal tube.

Nik shakes his head. "Haven't smoked since I was 13." Then his eyes fall onto the printed cannabis leaf on the container and he smirks. "Well, in that case... I could really use one of those." He looks around like a teenager about to smoke his first cigarette behind school, before he ads, "We should probably leave the premises for that, though."

Vasco raises an eyebrow but follows Nik toward the next bench. "And that makes a difference?"

Nik's laugh echoes around the empty courtyard. "Unfortunately, it does. We are no longer on private property owned by a man who would love any excuse to get rid of me, and I'm not sure he'd stop at jail time."

"Sounds like you were right when you said you needed this." Intrigued, Vasco lights the joint and takes a first draught, before handing it to Nik.

Vasco watches as Nik draws in the smoke, closes his eyes, then slowly exhales through his nostrils.

"13, ey?"

Nik's eyes open but Vasco can't make out their expression. "Early bloomer," Nik deadpans. When he continues to speak, there is an undertone in his voice that Vasco can't quite figure out. "I didn't have the best group of friends. My early teenage years were rough. I'm glad I got a wake-up call before I was in too deep."

Nik's tone makes Vasco's chest tighten and prevents him from giving in to curiosity. Instead, he places a hand on Nik's arm. "Sounds rough. Sorry for bringing it up. I'm good at finding puddles to step in."

Nik waves a hand. "Don't worry about it. There's a lot of puddles to step into." And then, as if realizing how sad that statement had sounded, he adds in a more cheerful tone, "So, why are you avoiding the never-ending fun of non-profit fundraising galas?"

The smoke catches on Vasco's throat when he can't stop the sarcastic laugh in time. He coughs, holds up a hand. A few coughs and throat clears later, his voice is rough but he squeezes out an answer. "It is impossible to strike a balance between sober enough to look like a picture-perfect accessory and drunk enough to be able to bear it."

Nik faces him, his expression suddenly sober. "Ah, a fellow accessory to greatness. Welcome to the club of lonely pretty boys."

"Pretty, ey?" Vasco asks, then mentally kicks himself.

Nik's eyes sparkle when he responds. "I know I clean up nice, so you are clearly not questioning the label applied to me. Which means: You haven't been told you're pretty often enough."

Because I'm not. And, in a moment of vulnerability, he repeats it out loud. He isn't sure if it's the night sky, the effects of the weed, or the fact that the man next to him is a perfect stranger.

Nik turns to face him, all of his attention on Vasco. The almost-black eyes drill into him, as if they can see through his skin. "I wish I could fake confidence as well as you seem to. But seriously—" Nik places a hand on Vasco's knee. "You don't need to fake it. I can't say you clean up nice, because I've only seen you in this." Nik's eyes give him an intense once-over that makes him feel... seen. He shivers when Nik looks him in the eyes and finishes, "I have a feeling you would look handsome in anything."

"If I'd known I would have to deal with compliments, I might have pretended I didn't see you earlier," he jokes, unable to do anything else.

"Clearly, you don't get enough of those," Nik states. When Nik's hand leaves Vasco's knee, it leaves a coldness behind that seems disconnected from the chill of the night air.

Vasco leans back again and whispers, "Maybe," before he can overthink it again. "Thank you, Nik."

Nik laughs in a way that makes the dark eyes light up like the stars in the sky above and Vasco relaxes.

They sit in silence, share the joint, and look at the night. When Vasco offers Nik the final draught, Nik finishes the join, squashes it under his feet, picks it up and carefully places it onto the bench next to him.

Vasco's grin is unstoppable when he realizes Nik doesn't want to leave the trash—not even the compostable remains of paper and hemp. Nik follows his gaze to the butt and shrugs. "I don't want to inspire others to leave cigarettes and other trash. They don't know it's just plants."

Vasco barks a laugh. Nik's wounded look makes him present his palms. "Sorry, I'm not making fun of you. Sorry. I promise. It's just..." He searches for the right words. "It's just that I have said almost those exact words so many times."

"And no one has ever understood the logic?" Nik finishes hesitantly, half question, half statement.

Vasco points a finger at Nik. "Exactly that."

Vasco usually carries an old candy box as a sort of portable ash tray but the slim-fit suit's pockets would make him look like a hamster trying to stuff too much broccoli into his cheeks, so he left it behind. Now, part of him wishes he had it with him. Nik would like it.

They share what Nik calls war stories about their fight against smokers who leave their damn cigarettes everywhere and how they can barely keep up with picking up what others discard without care, and

Vasco forgets about his duties inside until movement by the entrance makes them both turn.

The woman his mothers introduced earlier leans against the open door, her ball-gowned figure silhouetted against the light from the entrance hall.

"Duty calls."

The laughter on Nik's face is an echo for a split second, before it falls off, and he gets up. He squeezes Vasco's shoulder with a hand before walking away with a final, "It was a pleasure to meet you, Vasco." The pronunciation of his name is the closest to correct he has ever received from a non-native speaker. He smiles but it falters when he watches Nik walk toward the entrance hall. He joins the woman, and with an arm around her, follows her inside.

Duty calls.

I need to pretend

With every step Nik takes toward Percy, the night air seem to drop a few degrees, to get a little heavier. *Not everyone has the luxury to be an idealistic dreamer like you.*

"Hey," she greets him. Her voice is gentle, but he can't even look at her. He places a hand at the small of her back, and guides her inside. He doesn't say a word, as they climb the stairs, every step heavy and reluctant.

"Nik," she starts again, and he pauses mid-step. "Would you look at me, please?"

It takes his everything to turn and face her. When his eyes find hers Nik sees the sadness there, the guilt she must feel at her words.

She opens her mouth, closes it again, swallows hard, and reaches up to cup his cheek in her hand. Nik barely feels the touch. He's not here. In his mind, he's walking back down the stairs, and out into the night.

Her apology pulls him back to the moment. "I'm sorry," she says, and he knows she means it. "I shouldn't have said what I did."

He leans into her touch a little, her fingers warm against his face. "Nik," she starts again. "I need to pretend I give a shit about this fucking gala, but please, Nik, we need to talk."

He shrugs, nods, still doesn't speak. A little spark of hope is rising inside his chest, hope he doesn't even dare acknowledge.

Before he can answer, her face shifts to something behind him, and he feels someone standing there. "I'm sorry," she mumbles again, places a kiss on his cheek—the usual tip-toeing rendered unnecessary by her heels—and walks away.

"It's an honor to meet you sir," she simpers, and he turns to find her professional-as-fuck smile turned to 11 at a tiny man. Tailored tux, boulder hat, a fucking monocle. When were they? 1820? The quirky look identifies the man as Reginald Bold. The short man almost chuckles his monocle off his face, and holds out a fragile-looking hand. "Regi Bold. The honor is all mine, Miss Miller."

Simmons, he corrects in his head, but holds his tongue. Instead, he pulls out his phone and calls an Uber. When he reaches the courtyard, the benches are empty, and Nik feels more alone than he has in years.

All smiley-pancakes

Vasco kisses Ella's cheek, as he accepts the offered backpack. "Thank you, thank you. You are the best sister ever. Thank you!"

Ella laughs, bright sunshine even at 7.45 am. "Love you, too, bro. Now, go!"

He turns and rushes down the street, while throwing his backpack over his shoulder. He's so fucking late to class. How is he always late?

And who plans a fucking fundraiser for a Sunday night? Do rich people not work on Monday morning? Well, probably not. They probably have vacation days out of their asses and don't give a shit.

He dodges a grandma bent over her walker with a mumbled apology, and speeds up to a sprint. He slides into the closing train door at the last second, and collapses onto the seat right next to him. His breaths are labored, and he is hot, so hot. Running is definitely not his sport.

Okay, sport is not his thing. Fine. He's out of shape and he knows it. He leans his head against the seat when his pocket vibrates. It's a text from Ella.

Did you make the train?

He pants through his grin, as he responds, **Barely.**

You're trying not to die from a heart attack on the train, aren't you?

He scoffs, and types, **It's not *that* bad.**

He looks down at his still heavily rising and falling chest where a few extra pounds have started to accumulate.

Don't daydream all class, Ella sends back. He groans, actually audibly groans, before he remembers he's on a train full of people. He digs his headphones out of his backpack, and realizes how loud the train is at this time, when the sounds fade away by the wonders of noise-cancellation.

He shouldn't have told Ella. He should have kept his stupid mouth shut. But Ella had a way of getting information out of him, and when she had threatened to eat the breakfast she was cooking for him herself, unless he told her why he was all *smiley-pancakes,* as she'd put it, Vasco had spilled the beans.

He catches himself just before his brain dives into another rendition of meeting a perfect stranger at a fundraising gala he had tried to get out of for weeks.

You are the worst, he sends to Ella. He makes sure to include a purple devil—technically, it's an imp—emoji for emphasis. His train gets delayed, but the bus he has to catch after is even more late, so he arrives at the stop at the exact time the bus hits the curb with a front tire. Shouldn't bus drivers know their vehicles?

It becomes apparent quickly, that this particular bus driver has either never gone to bus-driving school or doesn't give a rat's ass about his bus. Vasco holds onto the loop attached to the ceiling for dear life, but still gets tossed around a bit at every turn. He bumps into people. People bump into him. And he adds layer and layer of odor to his own sweatiness.

When he walks into the lecture hall, he throws his backpack onto the floor, and bumps fists with Jesus, Gippy, and Diego, when their professor opens the door at the bottom of the lecture hall and walks in.

No ten minutes later, the professor's voice drones on far below him. The rows of students are tied between those drooling on closed notebooks and those immersed in their own screens. Next to Vasco, Jesus is playing *Guild Wars 2*, because the man has no fucking shame. They aren't even in the last row. Behind them, at least four people are following the little *asura's* attempts to beat up a much larger cave troll. Gippy pokes a snoring Diego in the side, before returning to his own distraction.

Vasco's hands are on top of his keyboard where he is reading a paper on the effects of bottom-trawling on the global climate.[2] It's not the same as playing MMORPGs[3] in class. His distraction is related to the subject matter—kinda.

Bullshit, he admits to himself. He isn't even reading the damned paper so much as staring at the screen where it's pulled up. Maybe he should be playing video games, after all. Staring at a paper without taking in a single word definitely ins't helping anyone.

He tries to listen to the professor and gets a few lines about something called a Hairy Anglerfish that he is sure would be super interesting if it wasn't presented in a voice that could be used as anesthesia for dental appointments.

And staying awake is even worse today, because they got home late, and he found sleep even later. He thinks of a few select punishments for the inconsiderate rich fuck who chose the date of the gala like enrolling in an 8 am class with Mrs. Monotone or walk on *Lego* for the rest of his life.—or better eternity. He accepts defeat and closes the paper. Scientific writing hasn't been known to wake people up, exactly.

He digs his palms into his eyes, but no amount of yawning or caffeine will keep him awake today—and considering the coffee in his stainless-steel mug is his third cup, that's saying something. It took the joint forces of all of his sisters to get him out of bed this morning. Fucking fundraiser.

And with that, he's back on the fundraiser. Or rather, he's back to thinking about Nik.

I have a feeling you'd look handsome in anything, are the words he can't forget. Okay, he also can't stop thinking about that tattoo that peaked out of Nik's sleeve. Or those eyes that were so moody and dark when they met, stars in the sky sparkles when Nik laughed, and an unreadable abyss when Nik walked away.

Duty calls, he had said, and there had been no warmth left in his voice, nothing left but rough ice.

Over and over, he watches Nik walk toward the woman, place his hand on her lower back. Nik had looked so hurt when Vasco had seen them talking at the top of the stairs. It had cost him a lot to keep walking. His helping-people complex really would get him into trouble one of these days. But the thing is, helping Nik wasn't all Vasco wanted to do to those broad shoulders and that first-rays-of-summer smile.

But he isn't thinking about Nik. He is paying attention to this lecture, damn it. Which, apparently, is ending, because Jesus is logging out of his account, and shutting his laptop.

He stuffs his own things into his bag, and joins his friends on the way out of the lecture hall. It really had been worth the hour-long commute. Yeah, totally worth it. He has half a mind of going home, but instead suggests a detour through the cafeteria to grab coffee number four and a protein bar. He has already missed one class in everything but physical presence, and doesn't have time to miss any more. He'll already have to figure out what the stupid anglerfish thing might have to do with his Physics 101 class.

Diego and Jesus are deep in a conversation about the merits of biodegradable plastics, and Vasco puts off asking his friends. Though he has a feeling at least Gippy will know. The little fucker had the impossible superpower of listening to any lecture while reading dense books Vasco doesn't even understand the titles of. And somehow, Diego can snore with an ear on the lecture. Impressive, really.

It also makes him feel like he isn't smart enough to hang out with them. Diego makes a fart noise with his hands in a very mature response to getting insulted by Jesus, and Vasco stops feeling inferior. He bumps a shoulder into Gippy's bony frame, and they all laugh.

Vasco missed the joke, but he doesn't care. These are his people, and he would worry about his never-ending todo list later.

Five letters

Nik sits in the living room surrounded by bottles of pills and is halfway through sorting out next week's supply when Percy stumbles into the living room in an oversized shirt that had once been his. Her eyelids are heavy, her skin even paler than usual.

They exchange a weak smile as she walks past him before she closes the bathroom door behind herself.

He cleans up the battlefield of medication strewn across the cushions, cleans two cups, and has prepared coffee for Percy and tea for himself by the time she returns from the bathroom with her hair in a towel turban, worn-out jeans, and one of her own shirts.

"Good morning," he says in what he hopes is a neutral tone.

She takes a sip of her coffee, as she lowers herself onto the couch. With her cup in her lap, she sits cross-legged, her side against the backrest. He knows she hasn't forgotten about last night.

"You wanted to talk," he states when she doesn't speak.

She nods, drinks some more coffee, pulls her leg into her chest, and rests her chin on her knee. But she doesn't say a fucking word. He wants to give her time, space, whatever she needs. He inhales the scent of his tea and takes a careful sip to avoid pressuring her. Fragments of emotions play on her face in a movie he cannot interpret.

"Nik, I..." she starts. She closes her mouth, begins again.

It is too much. He can't take it anymore. He hasn't been able to sleep, wondering what she wanted to talk about, what he *needed* to talk about. He has gone through a million versions of this talk. They've had versions of the conversation he expects to follow for years. He can't take another round.

He tries to wrap his head around the right way to say what he knows he needs to say, has needed to say for years, but the words won't form sentences.

"Do you feel forever about me?" he blurts out after a long while. He wants to take the words back the moment they are out there, somehow soften the blow. He bites his lip instead, watches his wife's face.

"Nik, I..." she says again. He doesn't need her to say it. But he has a feeling she might need to hear herself speak the words, so he waits. She runs a face through her hair, takes another draught from her cup, and sets it down on the coffee table, before looking back up at him.

"I haven't felt forever about any of this in a long time," she finally admits and he feels a decade of weight fall off his shoulders. He watches as truth reaches her, as her face loses tension held so long it has left first signs of wrinkles. But he lets her talk. "I didn't want to see it. I didn't see it. I really didn't. Not until yesterday." He kneads his hands in his lap to keep himself from reaching out to her. "I love you, Nik. I have always loved you. That that might not be enough has been dawning for a while, but I didn't see it, not really. Not until last night."

A single tear rolls down her cheek, and he wipes it away with his thumb. "It's okay, Cheeks."

"No, Nik. It's not fucking okay. How often have we had 'the talk?'" She puts air quotes around the words. "You've tried to break up with me for almost a decade now."

He wants to object, to tell her he has been all in. But he knows it would be a lie—and so does she. So, instead, he shuts up and listens.

"I hurt you last night. I know I did. You hurt me, too. You didn't mean to. But when you acted as if—" Her lip trembles, and he feels his chest tighten. "When you acted as if I wasn't—" She pauses, hesitates, then tries again. "I know how much you hate my father, and you have every reason to. My father, he, it's... I am not my father. You know how much I hate what the company does to this planet. You know. But yesterday, I wasn't sure you remembered."

Tears roll down her cheeks in hot trails. He opens his arms, pulls her into his chest. "Come here, Cheeks. I'ts okay. It'll be okay. I'm sorry I hurt you."

He holds her, his chest trembling with silent sobs, as her tears soak his shirt.

"No, it is definitely not okay. I shouldn't have lashed out," she says, voice muffled by his body. "I knew you didn't mean it. But you make me feel like I am part of the problem. I *feel* like part of the problem a lot of the time, like a fucking hypocrite. It's not like I am stopping my father from exploiting."

He strokes a hand over her head, kisses the top of it. "You aren't a hypocrite. You know you are doing what you can."

She sits upright, her eyes fierce. "It's not enough. I need to do more, be better."

He smiles at her. It is a sad smile, but she returns it nonetheless. "And you will," he says gently. She turns and leans against him. They sit like that for hours, comforting each other through the hurt as if they aren't the source. He hasn't felt this close to her in years. And for a moment, he thinks it is reconciliation, before he remembers this is the end.

"Nik?" she says when the lights begin to fade outside. He grabs his phone to turn on the lights, but she stops his hand. "Don't, please." He sets the phone down. "I don't feel like seeing the world right now."

He holds her tighter, and asks, "What do we do now?"

She digs her face into his arms. "You've changed a lot over the past decade, Nik. I've worn you down."

He shakes his head. "This isn't all on you."

She sinks into his embrace. "You used to be so fucking positive. It used to drive me insane, but it's also what made me fall in love with you.

I didn't notice that version of you had vanished. I should've seen it, but I didn't. Not until yesterday when I saw you with that guy."

His heart beats strongly in his chest, and they both know it's not for her. His heart hasn't been beating for her in a long time.

"You should be with someone who makes you light," she says after another moment. Nik's mind goes back to Vasco, but he doesn't get time to process this fact before Percy's phone makes them both jump.

Buzz. Buzz.

Her phone buzzes from somewhere on the couch, and she digs around for it. When she can't immediately locate it, Nik sits her up and begins to dig around for it, as well. After some struggles, he holds it out to her.

"Yes, hello?"

He face is screwed up in concentration, but there is no trace of tears in her voice. Percy has always been able to snap back to professionalism at an impressive speed. Someone on the other end of the line asks, "Miss Miller?"

She sits more upright, and asks with a fake smile on her face. "How can I help you?"

A sigh sounds before the voice speaks again. Nik can't make out most of the words, but the fragments he does hear make him tense. When she gets up, she sways, and he is on his feet to steady her. With his arms around her hip, he waits for her to finish the call.

"I'm on my way," she finally says, and hangs up the phone. "My father's had a heart attack. He's stable but weak."

She leans into Nik and buries her face into his chest for a moment, before letting him stir her back onto the couch. He grabs items with little thought: her purse, his wallet, to sets of keys. "I'm driving," he announces when he returns to the living room.

THE AGREEMENT HANGS unspoken between them like ellipses. Their end dragged out, because he will always be there for her, no matter the cost to him. He will go through this with her, because she cannot do it alone.

Percy sits pale and quiet on the passenger seat as he drives toward town. The seat feels all wrong. He doesn't drive often, doesn't even think of their car as his. Most of the car is still half-adjusted to his wife, but he doesn't have time to fix things now.

He places a hand on her leg, squeezes though he knows the gesture won't bring much comfort, and drives.

They arrive at the hospital where they get priority treatment from the moment the receptionist hears the name Steward Miller. A doctor talks to Percy within minutes, and they get led to a waiting room that makes Nik angry despite the circumstances. Yes, his wife's father has had a heart attack, and he is more worried about the injustice of the American medical system.

At least, no one would be drilling in the Arctic. He reprimands himself for being an ass. The man isn't even dead yet.

Percy's head rests in his lap, and he strokes the hair out of her face as they wait. It's not until his stomach growls that Percy moves at all. "You're hungry," she states.

"It doesn't matter," he answers, and it doesn't. Not to him. Not now.

It's another hour before a doctor in dark blue scrubs and a cap enters the room. Nik knows what they will hear, before the man opens his mouth.

Steward Miller, leader of the Bold oil empire, is dead.

Percy doesn't need to ask for his arm around her, as they follow the man to a room at the end of the floor. He hovers in the door while she kisses her father's forehead, whispers good-byes into his ear, and holds his hand for the last time.

He is there to catch her, when she sinks against his side on the way out. He hugs her to his left while he fills out paperwork at a nurse's desk. He kisses the top of her head when he leads her back to the car.

He half-carries her into their house and heads for her room, but she stops him. "No, Nik. I can't. I can't rest. I need to…"

He shushes her, but lets her go. "You need a moment."

She throws up her hands. "I need a million moments, but I won't get them now."

Her face is determined, and he knows he won't change her mind, so instead, he offers, "How can I help?"

She shakes her head. "I won't let you."

He takes her face into his hands, kisses the bridge of her nose. "Of course, you will. I'm here for you."

The next days are a blur. Percy is at the office more often than she has been in years. And Nik can't help, not really. He stays home, works while she is gone, takes care of the household and Marvin, and doesn't complain.

THEY DON'T TALK ABOUT *them* again until a few days after the hospital. It's Percy who brings it up. Nik had assumed that things would just go back to normal, the way they always did. It had almost felt normal over the past days.

Almost.

But if Nik pauses to evaluate the situation, things aren't normal at all. A decade of habits are hard to break, so there are a few almost-kisses that end with someone turning away, and both of them pretending nothing happened. Then there are the million little things that have changed. With Percy at the office, Nik has time to think. Without the pressure of keeping up a marriage, neither of them feels like fighting over chores or errands or opinions that don't matter anymore.

On day five, the night after the funeral, they sit on the couch again, Marvin curled up between them, his snout in Nik's lap. There's a stack of folders next to Percy on the couch, and her fingers fidget with a piece of paper.

"Thank you for helping me through the last few days. I don't know if I'd been able to do it without you." He is certain she has rehearsed whatever it is she needs to tell him. "I'm sorry for being home so little. There were things I had to take care of, things I had to get the ball rolling on before the—" She falters but pushes through. "—funeral."

She slides a hand over the cover of the topmost document folder, before continuing. "I know everything between us has been a little up in the air over the last few days."

He waves a hand. "It doesn't matter, Perce."

She shrugs. "Actually, Nik. It matters a lot. You shouldn't have to take care of the wife you just broke up with. That's not how this works. But it's who you are, and I am grateful for your support." Percy straightens her *Mt. Permafold*, and pushes the piece of paper in between. Nik knows it is to stop herself from fidgeting. "I have one more thing to ask of you."

I'll do it, hangs on his lips, but he bites his cheek and waits for her to explain.

"You know how much I've been struggling with everything at the company, and I have a plan. But, to make it happen, we'll need to keep pretending for a little while longer." He opens his mouth but she makes a tutting sound, and continues. "No, wait. Let me finish, please."

He leans back. She talks, and with every word she says, his jaw seems to want to drop lower. Whenever he manages to come up with a flaw or a question, she addresses it immediately. He feels like the recipient of one of her kick-ass presentations.

When she is done, her eyes shine with a fire that he hasn't seen in years. "What do you think?"

Now that it is finally his turn to speak, his brain refuses comprehensive sentences. His thoughts are racing through every worst-case and even-worse-case scenario. But he's grinning when he answers her, "I'm in. Let's change the world, Cheeks."

She grins back at him, her mouth curled in the crooked way she only lets herself show in private, the one that makes her the most beautiful woman in his life.

She shuffles the document folders in her lap, finds what she is looking for, and hands him a purple folder.

"What's this?"

The smile on her face falters, uncertainty mixed in. "I think you should have these in case anything goes wrong or you change your mind or whatever." He frowns, but doesn't interrupt. "I asked Larry to draw up divorce papers for us. I signed them this morning."

He takes the folder, opens it, and finds a stack of papers with little sticky tags on a few. Seeing Percy's signature underneath is a punch of reality. He knows they aren't handing them in any time soon, but he now has them. He can sign them, make it count, any time he wants.

"I asked him to divide everything except for the company equally between us. I would have included the company, of course, but it would make everything so much more complicated, and—"

"I understand. Don't worry about it, Cheeks."

Larry was their friend and lawyer. Nik trusted him—and he trusted his wife. He should probably stop thinking of her like that, though. Well, if they were going to keep pretending, he would have a lot of time for the concept to sink in. *Ah shit.* He's been quiet for too long, so he meets her eyes and thanks her.

When she sighs, he adds, "Are you okay? With all of this, I mean?"

"I will be."

He knows the feeling. He knows what they are doing is the right thing. But none of that keeps it from hurting.

"What's in the other folders?" he asks, mostly in search of distraction.

"It doesn't matter. Plans for proposals, information about board members, corporation structures—nothing you want to see." She sets the folders aside before holding out the crumpled piece of paper she fidgeted with earlier.

He raises an eyebrow, takes the paper, and opens it. It's a phone number and a five letters: **Vasco.**

Buzz buzz

The stench of student life hits Vasco when he opens the door to his apartment. He walks from window to window and pulls them open before even taking off his backpack.

Fuck, man. You are a mess.

He throws his backpack onto his bed, swears again, picks it up, and hangs it on the hook inside his closet door. It's time to grow the fuck up and get to cleaning. Now.

He fishes his phone out of his pocket and scrolls through Spotify until he lands on a Bob Marley playlist that begins with a *One Love / People Get Ready* medley.

Okay, first, laundry. He can let the load run while he cleans the rest. He snaps up the clothes littered across the room like fall leaves. He balls each item up and aims for the laundry basket through the open bathroom door. He's semi-successful, so he picks up the items around the basket, before heading to the basement.

Feeling accomplished, he returns to his kitchen, and pours dish water. His phone buzzes as soon as the gloves are on—and wet, of course. Already losing momentum, he ungloves one hand and reads.

Hi Vasco. This is Nik–

It's from Nik. Nik!

His skin prickles and a smile tucks on his lips. He gives up lying to himself about reliving their meeting all week, and responds.

Hola Nik.

Was that the right thing to say? When has he forgotten to text? He shakes off the feeling that he should add more and is half-way through gloving up, when—

Buzz buzz.

I've been thinking about you.

He would swear his heart skipped a beat. He know it's anatomically unlikely, but he would still swear. Now what? Damn it, he still hasn't figured out this whole flirting thing. He blames his mothers. If he hadn't spent his rebellious teens pretending to be straight to spite them, he might have a bit more experience with this shit.

Meaningless relationships with girls then and equally meaningless hookups with strangers in bathrooms later didn't exactly prepare one for the real stuff. And he decided about three days ago that he wants the real stuff–okay four or five, maybe even the moment he met Nik.

He hadn't let himself want the real stuff. Not since Michael had crushed his first attempt at a real relationship under his ridiculous cowboy boots.

Three dots appear on the screen, disappear, reappear, and disappear again. He's taking too long. Unable to think of anything smart of witty, he answers, **Me too.**

The dots stop bouncing, and he imagines Nik pausing to read. He sets the phone down on the counter, plugs it in to keep the screen from falling asleep, and gloves up one hand.

Buzz. Buzz.

I don't know how any of this works, so I'm just going to say it: Would you like to have a drink?

His dishes forgotten, he picks up the phone with the glove-free hand, and responds, **Yes,** before his brain catches up to his actions. What about the woman? Hadn't that been the woman on the stage? Persephone Miller, *fucking* princess to the Bold oil empire or whatever you call the daughter of the richest man in the nation. Or rather, the man who used to be the richest man in the nation.

He doesn't even try to put on a glove, because he is too busy staring at the screen, watching the fucking dots.

Fair warning: Things are pretty complicated.

He laughs, and responds. **I'm in. You can explain then.**

He writes, deletes, and rewrites **When can I see you?** a couple of times, before settling on: **When and where?**

He thinks about the options and wonders about the woman again. Is he about to become the *other woman* in this scenario? But he keeps returning to **Things are complicated** and forces himself to trust. Can you force trust? It would have to do, for now.

Are you free tonight?

With a look around the room, he throws his gloves next to the sink, leans back against the counter, and types: **Yes.**

He looks at the single word, repulsed by his lack of eloquence, and adds, **I can't wait.**

This is going to sound so fucking weird, but would it be okay to meet at your place?

He gasps, swallows hard. Without the laundry all over his place, some random clutter and Mt. Dishmore are the worst offenders. He checks the clock, straightens his shoulders, and types, **I can make that work.**

He prays that Nik doesn't suggest an early time and sighs in relief when he reads the message: **Great, meet you at 8?**

Vasco checks the time again, and knows that panic will have to carry him through straightening out the mess around him.

See you then. 2419 St. Elmo Dr., Apt. 1.

If he wants the apartment presentable to visitors—no, worse, a date—in less than three hours, Marley won't do it, so he pull up the app, and a playlist starting with *Ain't No Rest for the Wicked* sounds from the speaker.

Head bobbing along, swagger in his step, he pulls the gloves back onto his hand with a satisfying snap, and gets to work. This weekend was setting out to be a lot more interesting than anticipated.

Vasco is throwing cutlery into a drawer when the doorbell rings. Without checking the peep hole, he opens the door, and steps back. He catches the shy smile that makes Nik's short beard stand up a little, before his eyes are pulled down to the handsome Australian Shepherd mix panting happily next to Nik's thighs—a very familiar-looking Australian Shepherd.

"Hold on," he says without even a preliminary hello. "I know that dog."

He kneels in front of Marvin—Nik texted an hour ago to ask if he could bring his dog—and slowly moves a fist toward the dog's nose. Marvin sniffs his knuckles, before licking them. Vasco exchanges a look with Nik, before opening his hand, and petting Marvin between the ears.

Nik looks impressed when he asks, "Do you have a dog?"

"No, my parents collected children, not pets." He inhales sharply, and quickly adds, "That was a joke, sorry."

Nik laughs, but the confusion lingers in his eyes. "You'll have to explain that one at some point. But first: Hi!"

It is Vasco's turn to laugh. "Hey."

Nik stands outside his apartment door in a wide pair of fabric pants and a tank top that stretches over his muscles—and finally exposes the many black lines on Nik's arms. A fern is curled around Nik's lower arm, lines ragged as if drawn with charcoal. *Stop staring, you idiot,* he tells himself, as he steps back to let them in.

Nik looks at him from his chihuahua-print socks to the top of his head, and Vasco feels seen, the same way he did when they first met. When the earth-in-the-rain eyes meet his, he is sure his heart skips a beat. Fuck science. Nik walks past him, an uncertain smile pulling up one side of his mouth. Marvin is by his side at every step.

Nik runs his hands over his dreadlocks and pulls a headband from his wrist over them. Vasco wishes he could look this cool with this little effort. When Nik hovers in the hallway, Vasco remembers his manners and waves at the couch. "Make yourself comfortable."

Nik hesitates a moment, seemingly unsure where to sit, before settling down on the very edge of the couch. He points at the floor next to his feet, and Marvin rolls up there.

"You're the guy Marvin tried to eat at Pride parade, aren't you?" Nik asks when Vasco pulls up his desk chair, and sits across from Nik.

"It was more a very wet unexpected tongue kiss." He grabs two glasses from the coffee table and pours water. He sets one down in front of each of them.

"I was hiding from my wife that day," Nik admits, and Vasco knows it's a segue into an explanation. "Wife, eh?" he asks in an attempt at keeping things light.

Nik kneads his hands, and Vasco smiles. "Think some weed might help?"

"Sure can't hurt," Nik answers, and Vasco jumps from his seat. He turns in a half-circle before dialing in on his bedroom. On the way there, he remembers his fucking laundry, wet in the machine. He'll have to rewash the load tomorrow. Again. Well, at least, he forgot something Nik won't see. Ha.

With a tray in his hands, he returns to his living room. Nik looks lost on the edge of the couch, as if ready to run out of the apartment. In a moment of boldness, he sits down in the middle of the couch instead of the chair. Marvin opens an eye and lifts an ear, but relaxes when Nik doesn't move. In fact, Nik doesn't move or speak at all, and Marvin is back to snoring before Vasco has even fully sunk into the cushions.

"Are you nervous?" he asks, mostly to check that Nik is still responsive and not in some kind of shut-down or panic attack or whatever other brain things this might be. Vasco's mothers have taught him that everyone has baggage. He wants to learn about Nik's.

Nik unfreezes, almost meets Vasco's gaze, and answers with his eyes unfixed. "I don't really know where to start."

Vasco opens the jar and the sweet-and-sour of his favorite mood-lifting strain hits him. "How about you start by explaining why you are here if you are married to Persephone," he suggest while he grinds up the herbs and places them into a small bowl.

Nik flinches, and shock is spelled out on his face, before it vanishes just as quickly. "I wasn't sure you had puzzled that together yet." Nik looks on the verge of a question, but he presses his lips together instead.

Vasco closes the bowl and slots it into the vaporizer. "I'm not just my pretty looks," he jokes, and is rewarded with a bark of laughter from Nik. Traces of the emotion linger behind, as Nik leans his elbows onto his knees, and presses his face into his palms.

The vaporizer hums as it blows air into the attached balloon. Nik eyes the contraption curiously, but doesn't ask. Vasco pushes the mouth piece into the balloon, breathes in a lung-full of vapor, and hands the balloon to Nik. Nik inhales deeply, holds his breath with his eyes closed, before releasing a slow and steady stream of white cloud.

When Nik speaks, his voice's monotony rivals that of his physics teacher. "You are right," Nik concedes. "I am married to Persephone Miller, now the CEO of the Bold oil empire. But we are getting a divorce. It's complicated."

"So you said," he answers, and makes himself comfortable. "Tell me."

"We started dating right out of college. I had just gotten out of a shitty relationship. Her boyfriend had just moved to Australia. I was her rebound. She was mine." Once Nik starts talking, the words flow. "We never really dated, just went out with friends. Then, one night, she asked me to her house for a movie. We realized half-way through that it was playing in French. I had eyes (and ears, apparently) only for her, my little escape from the heart-break my previous relationship had left me with." Nik rubs a hand over his face, brushes his fingers through his dreadlocks. "Sorry, you probably don't care about any of this."

Vasco places a hand on Nik's shoulder. "It sounds like you need to tell someone. I'll listen."

"This is the weirdest first date ever," Nik groans. Vasco's heart leaps when the last doubts about what this evening is drains away. He laughs—okay, it's more of a very unmanly giggle—before admitting. "I haven't done this in a while."

Nik relaxes more with every lungfull, and by the time Vasco dumps the browned herbs into a jar, Nik has sunk into the cushions, one leg over the other in a figure four. He leans back, head resting on the couch, and closes his eyes. He continues, as if there had never been an interruption. "The next day, we tried to have sex, but it was her first time—not that I had much more experience, and I was so nervous. We made out instead, but it was still weird. We didn't try again for two weeks. When we actually managed, I lasted about thirty seconds."

Vasco laughs. "Been there."

"We tried to laugh about it. She was great about it, but it still made me feel inadequate. We figured it out after a couple of years, but by the time we did, everything else had fallen apart." Marvin twitches and half-barks in his sleep, and they exchange a grin, before Nik continues. "Her father hated me from the beginning. My family never liked her. We felt like Bonny and Clyde against the world. It was great for a while, but things started crumbling over time. It's like we were speaking different languages. But we also had fun, and things were mostly comfortable."

"When did you know you wanted it to end?" Vascos asks and places a hand on Nik's knee. Nik looks at his hand, and he almost pulls it away, before Nik's hand is on his and his chest explodes with shooting stars.

You and your feelings, man

Nik can't tear his eyes from Vasco's hand on his knee. When he squeezes Vasco's hand, his chest squeezes, too, and Nik feels like his heart might puke—and somehow that's a good thing, a feeling that tucks at the corners of his mouth until he is grinning like a cartoon idiot.

Vasco's warm touch anchors him as he tells his story. "The first time I tried to break up with her was two years into our relationship. But she said all the right things, and I stayed."

Nik feels Vasco's gaze on himself and looks up. Vasco's face is unreadable, a puzzle of different micro-emotions he cannot combine. "Did she manipulate you?" he asks.

Nik shakes his head without the slightest hesitation. "No, no. I don't think she even realized what she was doing."

"Did things get better after you talked?"

Vasco's touch is firm and comforting on his knee, so he makes sure not to shift his leg when he leans his head back. His gaze on the ceiling, he answers. "For a while. Things always got better for a while. We argued. We hurt each other. I wanted to leave. We talked. I stayed. Things got better for a few days, sometimes even weeks. But it never lasted.

"What changed?"

Nik lifts his head to meet Vasco's gaze, and tears try to fight their way out. "She saw me with you."

"You know it's okay to cry, right?" Vasco says. Nik's laughter catches in his throat, and an unflattering sound escapes his lips. The tears roll down his face, and he is crying, but while his chest is heaving with sobs, there's also laughter. When Nik calms down, the tears don't stop falling. "You and your feelings, man."

Vasco leans a little closer to Nik, "I grew up in a home where feelings are encouraged and shared."

Nik never lets himself cry where others might see. He's pretty sure Percy is the only person who has seen his tears since the age of eight when his father hit him for crying over his broken bicycle. But things are different with Vasco. Vasco doesn't seem to see vulnerability as a weakness.

"This is definitely the weirdest date ever," he says through another sob. And then Vasco's hand is leaving his knee, and he feels cold and exposed, until Vasco's fingers are on his face, tracing the line of his stubbled jaw. Vasco's palm comes to rest on his cheek, and Nik finds himself leaning into the touch.

It takes him a everything to pull back. Panic rises inside him when he sees the look on Vasco's face. He splutters in an attempt to explain. "No, no. Don't look at me like that."

Even after being hurt, Vasco waits for Nik to sort through his thoughts, and Nik is thankful for the patience. "I need to you hear me out before you do something you'll regret later."

"I wont' regret it. I can make my own mistakes, Nik." Vasco's voice is thick with something. Nik has no idea what it is, but he wants it gone.

"Vasco," he attempts. He chews his lip, and again Vasco gives him space to think, even now that someone as emotionally illiterate as Nik can see the pain he has caused. When his brain slots into place, Nik hears the words that come from his mouth without choosing them. "What I want more than anything right now is to kiss you." Vasco's eyes shoot from his own feet to Nik's face, and Nik has to grab the couch to prevent himself from kissing the man's face off. Instead, he says, "I can't. Not yet. I need you to understand what you are getting into."

Vasco looks ready to argue, but scoots back on the couch until his back is leaning against the arm rest on the other side, folds his arms over his chest, and smiles. He looks comfortable, as if this wasn't all weird and complicated. "Sounds like you are doing this for some stupidly noble reason, so I'll let you do what you need to do."

Nik wants to argue that he doesn't have to be so far away to listen, but his hand is still clenching the couch, and Vasco's hands are folded so damned tightly.

He tells Vasco about his conversation with Percy the day before, even shares their plan for the company. He knows he shouldn't be sharing it with someone he barely knows, but Vasco needs to understand.

When he is done talking, Vasco's jaw has given up fighting gravity, and he waits as Vasco's lips open and close like those of a goldfish in a bowl. "Say something," he says when he can't stand the silence for a moment longer.

"Wow," Vasco manages, before returning to his fish-gasps. Nik searches for more to say, to make the distance between them seem less far, less cold. His eye catches on a rip in the fabric, and he stares at it, until Vasco's milk-and-honey voice pulls him back. "Okay," is all Vasco says, before he is up and standing in front of Nik, pulling him to his feet. "Okay," he repeats, as he slides a hand around Nik's waist and pulls him closer.

"There's one more thing," Nik forces out, and Vasco groans in frustration. When Vasco growls—actually growls—Nik leans his forehead against his. "I've never kissed a man," he whispers against Vasco's cheek. He feels Vasco's smile. When Vasco asks, "Can I kiss you now?" he bobs his head. And then Vasco's lips are on his, and the world fades away.

Guapo

Kissing Vasco is nothing like kissing Percy. It's nothing like kissing any of the women he has kissed. Kissing Percy was like half-molten marshmallows at a campfire. Kissing Vasco is cinnamon and lemon over apple pie.

When Vasco pulls back, Nik follows, and Vasco's lips tighten over a smile, before they return to his. Nik slides a hand over Vasco's back, and pulls him closer. Vasco presses into Nik, kisses the side of his mouth, up his cheek, until his lips are next to Nik's ear. Nik feels his body tense. Immediately, Vasco leans back enough to see Nik's face and Nik is sure he will ask him what's wrong, but Vasco smiles at him, cups his cheek, and asks in a gentle tone, "What happened?"

"You never judge, do you?" Nik asks instead of a response. He leans into Vasco's hand on his cheek and Vasco strokes it with his thumb.

"I try not to," Vasco whispers.

"I don't like the feeling of hot breath on my skin. I'm sorry. I know they make it sound like this super sexy thing in books, but I just—" Nik shivers and looks down at Vasco's shoulder. Vasco places a finger underneath Nik's chin and gently guides him upward until their eyes meet again. He brushes a kiss onto Nik's lips, before saying, "You'll have to teach me."

Nik expects him to try again, to ask Nik to stop him if it's too much, the way Percy did. Well, the way Percy did once she stopped feeling personally insulted by Nik not liking her breath on his skin. But Vasco isn't Percy and Nik is only mildly surprised, when Vasco kisses his mouth instead.

Vasco pulls Nik onto the couch where they kiss until their lips are swollen, their breaths short and fast. Vasco tastes like hope.

Nik sits up, and Vasco turns to rest his head in Nik's lap. Nik's hand is in Vasco's hair before his brain catches up to his body. Vasco's hair is silky and soft, so Nik runs his fingers through it.

Vasco looks up at him with golden-brown eyes, and asks with a smile, "Is it different? Kissing men, I mean."

"It's different kissing *you*," he answers. "I don't know about *men*."

Vasco chuckles and places a hand on Nik's face. "You take things so literally."

Nik tenses again, and an apology escapes before he can stop it. But Vasco's thumb draws electric lines on his cheek, his jaw, his lips, and he knows Vasco isn't poking fun. Vasco's eyes are soft when he whispers, "Don't you dare apologize for that."

Nik barely swallows another apology, and is rewarded by Vasco pulling himself up and kissing Nik until they are out of breath again, and Nik can't even remember what he was worried about. When Vasco's lips are on his, it is easy to lose himself, to forget about the clusterfuck that his life is. It's like nothing Nik has ever experienced. But he is pretty sure that the difference has nothing to do with gender and everything to do with the handsome man in front of him.

"I was right, you know?" he says when Vasco sinks back into his lap. Vasco raises a dark eyebrow. "Well, technically... Ah, nevermind. You look handsome in anything."

Vasco blushes above a smirk. "Two samples enough to make that decision?"

"I already knew when I first saw you," Nik admits, and lifts Vasco up for another kiss.

They kiss; they talk; they kiss some more, and it is well past midnight when Vasco suggests a late-night snack. Nik watches as he dances through the kitchen in a flowery pink apron that looks fourth-generation, expertly avoiding a suddenly very awake Marvin searching for dropped scraps. Vasco twirls around to face Nik, places another kiss onto his mouth, before returning to the stove with a swing in his step.

Nik feels useless and keeps offering help, but with Vasco cha-cha-chaing through the small space, there isn't room to help, so Nik leans back against the counter. Vasco pulls him back to the present with quick check-ins on food preferences, but in-between confirming that he prefers corn tortillas to wheat and that veggies are all good, he looks around and takes in the space.

Vasco's place is a small one-bedroom apartment with well-used furniture that looks like most of it is hand-me-downs or flea-market finds. Every inch of the window sills is covered in plants, and Nik finds himself wandering around to inspect them until his eyes fall onto a stack of records in a corner.

"You still own real vinyl?" he asks.

Vasco is stirring vegetables in a large, scratched-up pan. "It's even more pathetic: I don't even own a record player to play them." He lifts the spoon to taste his cooking, before continuing. "My mama used to take me to this small record store by our house, and I would spend my pocket money on records every single month. Mom managed to get an old entertainment system with a record player the next Christmas, and I was in heaven."

"What happened to it?"

Vasco adds spices to the pan. "Cassette deck ate a tape from the library. Mama had to pay for the stupid cassette, and my entertainment system couldn't be saved." He walks toward Nik, holds out the spoon. "Try this."

Obediently, Nik accepts the offered food. "Fuck, that's good. *Chipotle* should give up and close their doors."

Vasco beams at him. "Chipotle is hardly a high bar to hit." When Nik wants to object, Vasco adds, "I know you gringos like your *Chipotle*."

The Rs roll off Vasco's tongue in a way that makes Nik reach out for his hand and pull him into his arms. "I like it when you speak Spanish—even if it's to insult me," he admits, and kisses the crooked smile on Vasco's face.

"Oh, guapo, calling you a white boy is hardly an insult."

Nik doesn't know what *guapo* means, but it doesn't matter. He would listen to Vasco read out the manual to a laundry machine in Spanish—or any language for that matter.

Vasco adds the heaven-sent grilled vegetables to the corn tortillas he roasted over the open cooktop flame and hands Nik a plate. "I'm afraid, I don't really own a dining table—or a dining room for that matter."

Nik looks around, and considers the coffee table and the kitchen counter, before sitting down on the floor with his back to the kitchen cabinets. "I'm not really a chair person anyway."

Vasco's eyebrows lift, but he slides onto the floor next to Nik.

"So, tell me, how is all of this supposed to work?" Vasco asks ten minutes later when he pushes his plate onto the kitchen counter above their heads.

Nik lets his head fall against the cabinet and groans. "I really wish we didn't have to talk or even think about that."

It's kinda my MO

Nik looks at home on the floor, harem pants spread over crossed legs, eyes closed, but Vasco sees his bare toes open and close, open and close, in an endless repetition.

"Not really first-date talk, is it?" Vasco says as he pushes himself to his feet, and holds out a hand for Nik. Nik opens his eyes, and takes it. Vasco pulls to help him up, and it feels like he is actually helping, though he has a feeling Nik is the one doing all the work.

"Don't really have a comparison," Nik says, and his cheeks flush pink.

"Wanna go for a walk?" Vasco offers, but Niks shakes his head, so Vasco leads him back to the sagging couch and fills another bowl with herbs. If they have to talk about this shit, they might as well be comfortable.

"We can't exactly be seen together, can we?" Vasco asks when Nik doesn't speak. "Not yet."

Nik stares at the wall opposite them. "I won't blame you if you—"

Vasco places a finger over Nik's lips. "Don't. I told you I'm in. So don't tell me to get out before it's too late or whatever. I'm in. I've been in since you first turned and looked at me outside that ridiculous fundraiser."

"I hate fundraisers," Nik says, and Vasco chuckles.

They hand the balloon around, refill it immediately, and Vasco feels a comfortable buzz in his mind that instead of clouding his thoughts leaves him able to think.

Nik groans his loudest yet and wipes both hands over his face. Marvin is by his side immediately, pressing a wet nose into Nik's face, licking his cheek. "I'm okay, Marv," Nik says, and pushes her back to the floor. He buries his face in Marvin's fur for a moment, before leaning back into the couch, and pulling Vasco against his chest. "Or at least, I will be," he whispers with his face in Vasco's neck.

Nik's beard is rough against his skin, but Vasco doesn't mind. He turns to kiss Nik, and Nik's lips find his. He has to force himself not to get lost in the contact. He sinks into Nik's chest, places his hand over Nik's and interlaces their fingers. Nik squeezes once, but slides his fingers out and around Vasco's hand instead. Vasco knows he is being taught how Nik prefers to hold hands. He tightens his grip around Nik's fingers and presses another kiss on his cheek.

"I don't want to go home," Nik says after a moment.

"Guapo," Vasco whispers, as he pulls Nik's head closer with a hand around his neck. He doesn't know what to say, how to make things better. He slides a finger over the side of Nik's neck, and a small sigh escapes Nik.

Vasco traces the lines of the muscles on Nik's arms, and waits for Nik to gather his thoughts. Nik nuzzles Vasco's neck, and Vasco slides his fingers into Nik's hair. After a very long pause, Nik finally says. "My wife—Persephone, I mean. Sorry." Nik's cheeks flush, and Vasco kisses the red blotches.

"I don't know how long you've been together exactly—" he says.

"Twelve years," Nik interjects.

"—but you'll need time to wrap your head around things."

"I know, but I hate it. I've pretended with myself for years, then with her and the world. I don't want to pretend anymore."

Vasco wants to help, to make things better, but he can't. Not for now. Not really. "How long do you think you'll need to keep pretending?"

Nik makes a sound somewhere between frustration and uncertainty. "I don't know. It's the worst part. I don't know how long I'll be stuck in this torturous limbo."

Vasco wants to ask if it will be days, weeks, or months, but he knows it would only make things harder for Nik. And making things harder for Nik is the very thing he is trying to avoid.

"We need to convince the board that she is not their worst nightmare—and that's hard enough for her, because, well, because she's a woman but not a housewife," Nik explains. "She has to walk the fine line between putting her work first all the time, working way too much, while also looking as if she fulfills the role they assign her in their minds." Nik is talking fast, and Vasco limits his reactions to nods and hm-hm sounds. "It's all these old white dudes, misogynistic pricks, racist assholes, just intolerant as fuck. If they find out she is getting a divorce, they will eat her alive. Christian values and such."

Nik is quiet for a moment, and Vasco considers saying something, but then Nik is off again, rambling on as if the words are forcing themselves out. "Ive been skipping steps my whole life. It's kinda my MO. PTSD at 9, petty theft at 12, quit smoking at 14. Marrying Percy right out of my first real relationship, right after I'd been dumped. We never even went on a date before I asked her to be my girlfriend. We just hung out with mutual friends a couple of times. Her feet were in my lap for most of the NYE party that year. Two days later, we were a couple. Fuck, I had to explain to her father that she was worth a damn the first time I was over there. First argument with her parents on day four of our relationship. And we got married to make it easier for her to go to Europe. Visa reasons." Nik scoffs, his voice still frantic, hands clenching Vasco's tighter and tighter. "Fucking romantic, isn't it." I followed her to Europe. We lived in the Netherlands for a while. I fell in love with Spain while exploring Valencia for a week while she was in important meetings for her father."

Vasco wants to ask about Europe, about Spain, most of all about Nik's feelings, but he just nuzzles his head against Nik's neck, and listens.

When we came back here, I felt lost. Rooted to the spot by her job, I felt caged. But the truth is, I was even more trapped by my own financial dependence. I skipped college to pursue a career in freelance journalism—and it even worked out for a couple of years. I was good at it. Fuck, I even got to speak in front of a couple hundred people plus more online once. It was a disaster, because Amy Whinehouse's death got announced half-way through my speech and half the tweets I was basing my talk on didn't show, because Twitter was down."

Vasco feels the laugh Nik releases, before he hears it, a deep roll in Nik's chest. His lips pull up, and he laughs with him. "I have so many questions," he laughs.

The laughter lingers in the muscles of Nik's cheeks for a while, before he continues talking. "I almost threw up right before the show. Then, the announcer person forgot my request for the introduction, and I had to improvise. I'm not very good at improvisation. There's even video of the disaster."

"Oh, I've got to see that at some point," Vasco announces, and turns to press a giant smooch on Nik's blushing cheek. Nik rewards him with a soft smile and a chuckle. "Over my dead body, babe."

Nik tenses, his eyes widening in shock. He presses his lips together, pulls them between his teeth, and Vasco puts him out of his misery. "I like it, guapo."

Nik releases his lips, and the corner of one side of his mouth twitches the tiniest bit. "Do you speak Spanish?"

"I do," Vasco answers. "But you are redirecting, and as much as I want to torture you with the video, I want to know more about your life." *I want to know everything about your life.*

Nik looks torn for a second, before he settles back down in the cushions, pulls Vasco into a tight embrace, and continues his story.

Vasco's heart beats faster when he hears how much of the tension and panic has drained from Nik's voice.

"Where was I? Right, the speech. I wrote a few articles for magazines, once for a small newspaper. I published blog post after blog post, and raised a little following. People paid me to teach them about writing, about how to take good photos to go along with the articles. Most of my students were a lot older than me." Nik is lost in thoughts for a moment, and Vasco lets him think. "Persephone's connections didn't hurt, but I did a lot of the hard work myself, and I am proud of what I achieved. But then 2020 happened, and suddenly my style of journalism took a back-row seat to click-bait titles about incidence numbers."

"I'm sorry, Nik," Vasco says.

"It's okay. I'll figure something out. I tried starting a podcast, and it's been working out okay, but I don't want to be a podcaster for the rest of my life."

"Of course, you'll figure it out, babe." He hadn't meant to use the pet name, but it had felt right, and he wasn't going to apologize for something that felt so fucking right.

"And now," Nik says with an air of resignation, "I am skipping all the steps with you."

"It's okay," Vasco says immediately, because it is. "It is okay."

Nik throws up a hand. "It should not have to be okay. I'm 31 years old. I've only been with three partners, slept with four people. I figured out I'm bisexual in my mid-twenties, because I never explored. I stumbled from my first real thing into a marriage, and it was easy to tell myself that my sexual orientation didn't matter, because I wasn't able to explore anyway. I felt more and more caged every day. It was like opening Pandora's box, all the thoughts I had pretended not to think spilling over into a life I grew to resent. It's not Percy's fault. I'm sorry, but it isn't. I wasn't available, not to her. She never stood a chance. And the worst thing is, I really loved her."

"Do you still?" he asks as gently as he can. He isn't worried, per se, but a small part of him needs to hear Nik say it.

Nik shakes his head. "I'm not in love with her. I don't think I ever really was. I loved her and, in a way, I still do. But we aren't meant for each other. I want her to be happy, but I can't give her that. And she can't give me what I need either."

Nik holds his breath until Vasco nods. "Okay."

"I'm sorry for pulling you into all of this," Nik says, and Vasco hears the guilt.

"When all of this is dealt with, I'll take you on as many dates as you want. We'll go through all of the steps, okay?"

"They'll be out of order, already are," Nik tries to convince him.

Vasco turns, throws his legs over one of Nik's and faces him. It's not comfortable, not at all, and his stupid thigh muscles will give up on him in about twenty-two seconds, so he makes the best of them, and kisses Nik full on the mouth, hard and slow. It takes Nik half a second to return the kiss, but when he does, Vasco sighs. Worth every bit of torture he is putting his legs through.

But when they break apart, he immediately collapses onto the couch. It's not graceful, not even close, and Nik laughs at the sight. It's not a mean laugh, and Vasco feels laughed with instead of laughed at, so he laughs along. He pulls Nik on top of him, and enjoys the weight of his body as they share another kiss.

Nik's tongue flits against his, and sparks explode in his spine, like fireworks in July. They get lost in each other, kiss until they are panting, out of breath, and Nik slides onto the couch next to Vasco. He puts an arm over Vasco's side, and his head onto his chest. "I could stay here forever."

"I want you to stay. Well, except for the part where the left half of my ass is falling off the couch."

They both laugh again, and Vasco is vaguely aware of how loud they must be at this time of the night—whatever the time is. Nik pushes him a little, and Vasco rolls off the couch, the unstable balance finally tipping. Nik's strong hand catches his hip just before it collides with the couch table. Nik pulls him back onto the couch, face to face, noses touching. "I've got you," Nik whispers, and a shiver makes the hair on Vasco's arms stand.

"For someone who has never been on a date, you've definitely got some moves," he laughs, and then he's kissing Nik again. Nik breaks contact after just seconds, and Vasco wants to pull him close again, but Nik's hand is on his chest, holding him back. Nik untangles himself from Vasco, and is pacing the apartment by the time Vasco has fully turned to face the room.

"Did I—" he begins, but Nik shakes his head with vigor. "Nope, you didn't do anything wrong. I just—wanna go for that walk after all?"

Vasco splutters, confused, as he sits up. "Um. Okay. I have no idea what just happened, but, um, sure."

Nik laughs, stops his pacing with obvious effort, and faces Vasco. "I'm sorry, man. This is ridiculous. I—" He holds up both hands, takes a deep breath, and tries again. "If you keep kissing me like that, I won't be able to control my dick for much longer. I'm walking off an impending erection over here."

Not for the first time, Vasco is surprised by Nik's blunt honesty, and it takes him a moment to react. Nik looks as if he is certain he should have just shut his face, so Vasco gets up, and walks over to him.

He smiles a one-sided smile he usually hides but doesn't want to hide from Nik, and puts his arm around Nik's waist.

"Not helping," Nik stammers, and Vasco can feel the hardness underneath the fabric pants. He grins, and instead of releasing Nik, presses into him, and pushes him toward the nearest wall. Nik's back hits the wall, and Vasco knows Nik is much stronger and could have stood his ground. But Nik let him, and Vasco feels his own want build. He kisses Nik until they are breathless, before he forces himself to push off Nik's chest with both hands. A moan of protest escapes Nik, but he lets Vasco go.

Vasco turns and breathes away his own erection, as he grabs Marvins' leash. "Walk. Now. Before we skip more steps."

Marvin runs up to him, tail wagging, and holds very still while Vasco hooks the leash. He grabs his keys from the hook by the door, and purposefully takes his time, before he faces Nik again. Nik's cheeks are still pink, but he smiles timidly, and nods when Vasco asks if he is ready.

They walk along the dark streets toward the park a few blocks away. Marvin walks between them, and they talk about little things. Nik tries to find Ursa major, and Vasco teaches him how to recognize it. Marvin runs around, catching sticks they throw, until the first light appears behind the trees, and the stars fade.

"Ready to go back?" he asks when they can't avoid the end of the night for longer.

Nik nods, shakes his head, shrugs. "Not really, but I'll have to."

When they get back to the apartment, Vasco pulls Nik in for a good-night kiss, okay, a few good-night kisses, and a good-bye kiss by the door, before Nik walks away, Marvin by his side.

When Vasco closes the door behind himself, he doesn't need the clock on the wall to tell him it's almost time for breakfast. He considers lying down to catch up on sleep, and he has half convinced himself that he deserves a rest and that it's Sunday after all when a voice that sounds a lot like Ella reminds him about the papers he has to finish before family dinner that night. So, he places a mug under his behated *Keurig* instead.

This is going to be a long day, but there is no doubt in his mind that getting to kiss Nik is worth all the yawns and desperate stretches in the world.

I thought you were joking

Nik has never seen the house this clean, probably not even when they moved in. He's on his third cup of mate, and as caffeine makes him go into squirelly productivity, he's been cleaning, well, everything.

He's hanging the towel back onto the hook by the fridge when Percy's door opens, and she emerges, half-dressed, but with a stack of files under one arm. Marvin dashes for her and licks her elbow even though she keeps walking.

"Good morning," she sing-songs, and Nik crosses his arms and leans against the wall, one eyebrow raised.

"The fuck are you so happy about?" he asks, wondering who the woman is and what she did to his wife, because this... this is definitely not Persephone Miller-Simmons.

"Wanna go to the gym together?" she asks, still in the chipper suddenly-a-morning-person tone." After lunch, maybe? I've got to finish these, but I really need a break, and I thought, maybe, well, unless it's weird. I'm sorry. Do you?"

Nick laughs at her, and she pouts, mock-offended. "Er... sure," he answers, before he can overthink the weirdness of it all. It's just a workout. And if they have to pretend to be happily married and all that shit, they might as well try this friendship thing. He still makes a mental note to text Vasco about it, so it won't feel like a secret.

"I'll let you know when I'm done. Probably around noon, okay?" Percy says, and is already halfway to the coffee-maker, when he agrees.

"I can make you coffee," he says. "You look—" He puffs out air. "Busy?"

She laughs, turns, hands him her mug. 'You are a life saver."

She walks past him, presses a peck onto his cheek, freezes, and starts stumbling backward. "I'm sorry, Nik. I didn't mean to."

He groans. "Don't worry about it. You've got more than a decade of habits to undo."

She splutters, her cheeks pink with shame. "Oh Nik. This is all—I don't know. This sucks!" She stamps a foot and throws her hands up.

"Of course it does," he says gently. "It all sucks ball." But this angry-dwarf-style temper tantrum doesn't make things better, so he adds, "But if we want even a remote chance to save the Arctic from your father's legacy—"

"I know. I know," she says and holds up a placating palm. "I know. I just really wish you didn't have to suffer through all of this."

She leans back against the counter, and takes in the room. He places her mug in the coffee maker, even though she is right next to it now, and presses two buttons. The ugly beeping sound only makes him flinch the tiniest bit.

"Thank you," she says very quietly. "I know how much you hate wearing suits."

"The dress shoes are worse," he counters.

"I'll text Isavella to see if she's working today," she says, slowly scanning their living room.

He hands Percy the cup and looks at her. "Isavella, eh?"

Percy's cheeks go from fading pink to blotchy red. She's biting her lips, and he is torn between thinking she's cute and not wanting to think it. She shifts awkwardly, and her gaze skits around the room in an obvious attempt not to look at Nik. He sees the moment in her eyes when she seizes the chance to deflect.

"Too much caffeine?" she chuckles with a nod toward the folded laundry in a basket on the couch. In an undertone, she adds, "Or too many endorphins?"

He watches, as she takes in their place, almost unrecognizable in its current state. He's not sure she's ever noticed his efforts. In her defense, the apartment is sparkling in a way that's hard to miss.

"It looks great, Nik." She smiles at him, and adds, "Thank you."

She drains the last of her coffee, and placed the mug next to the sink. A ring of brown liquid pools around its base.

Unable to deal with the gratefulness, and his mixed feelings about everything from the fucking cup staining the otherwise immaculate countertop to her blushing over someone who isn't him, he shrugs and mumbles, "It's no big deal," even though it has been.

"I need to finish this," Percy announces with a smirk, and she is halfway to her bedroom door, when he calls after her. "Don't think I didn't notice that you changed the topic. You can't avoid me forever."

She winks at him, and pulls the door shut behind herself. Marvin stands outside it with her nose almost touching the door. He picks up her mug, claps his palm onto his thigh for Marvin to join him, and cleans first the mug and then the countertop.

Percy texts him that she'll be ready in five, so he packs his gym bag, and heads toward Percy's room. The door is closed, and despite entering it unannounced a million times before, he hesitates. Should he knock?

Fuck it. He'll wait for her to come out, yeah. Best to avoid the issue. He turns and has taken one step when the door opens behind him. He halts mid-step and faces her. Percy is in her usual workout clothes: sports bra, loose tank top, and something between leggings and hot-pants that he has never quite been able to understand.

"Ready?" she asks, and heads for the door without waiting for an answer.

He shoulders his bag and follows.

They don't really talk on the way to the gym. Both of them take a few stabs at small-talk, but after twelve years of marriage, there isn't much left to say—and things are weird between them. Nik doesn't like it, but they are.

Isavella waves at them when they enter, and waits for them at the turnstile, one hand on the button to buzz them in. They have membership cards, and they could scan them, but they are here often enough that people know them.

"I haven't seen you in days, chica," she greets Percy with a grin, then reaches out a fist to Nik. Nik bumps it and hovers as Isavella hugs Percy, swaying from side to side like an excited puppy. Speaking of, Sparkles, the ridiculous Frenchie Isavella foster-failed, wobbles up to them and jumps up Nik's leg.

He bends down, and Sparkles drops onto his back for easy access. "Someone is greedy for belly rubs, aren't you?" he sing-songs in a weird baby voice that annoys even himself.

Isavella gestures for them to wait, and runs toward the staff-room door. They hear her yell for someone to take over the front desk, and Nik looks at Percy. "You should ask her out," he says for what feels like the millionth time.

"You've been telling me," she answers, the first tiny specs of a blush forming. "I thought you were joking."

He laughs. "So did I."

Isavella takes off her staff shirt and throws it behind the counter. She pulls her dark hair into a high ponytail before throwing an arm around each of them and leading them to the obstacles. "So, what am I torturing you with today?"

She does indeed torture them, but Nik doesn't mind. A good workout has always helped his mind, even lifted some of the constant brainfog he's battled for years.

"Don't give up yet!" Isavella yells, but he collapses onto the floor, and pants. "Nope, not happening."

He drags himself into a sitting position, and watches Percy and Isavella vault a wall twice their height. They grin at each other and high-five, before sliding down the pole at the side of the wall.

He lets himself fall back, and stares at the ceiling, one ear on Percy and Isavella, too exhausted to do anything but lie around. He lets his head tilt to his side, just in time to push Sparkles and his very wet tongue away. With the motivation of a teenager asked to do his homework, Sparkles gives up immediately, and rolls into a tiny ball at Nik's shoulder.

"You are one weird dog," Nik says, as he pats the stupid thing.

After a moment, Percy and Isavella sit down on either side of him, and pull him into a seated position. Sparkles dashes around Nik and straight into Isavella, then tries to climb up her thigh. He shakes from apparent exertion, and then his butt is on the floor. Isavella takes pity and lifts him into her lap.

"Letting your wife beat you? Lazy ass," Isavella teases, and he half-heartedly shows her the finger.

When he first got to the gym, he could barely walk up the stairs to the entrance, let alone make it across a set of monkey bars. When Isavella found out about his aching joints, his weak muscles, his dizziness, she didn't mollycoddle him. She pushed. And he is thankful for it. She might be barely more than 5 feet tall, but Isavella Maduro is the reason he can lead a pretty normal life. Well, her and a bunch of painkillers, supplements, and drugs.

"I need a shower," Percy announces, and Isavella gets up with her. Nik nods, and holds out his arms. They pull him to his feet, and his legs are shaky, but after a moment, he steadies himself, and lets go of their hands.

Isavella's hand is on Percy's back, when they vanish into the women's locker room, and Nik smiles to himself. Percy should really ask her out.

He digs his phone out of his gym bag, and texts Vasco, **Can I come over later?**

He waits a few seconds, but no dots appear, so he locks his phone up, and heads for the showers. He considers taking a cold shower, but chickens out—as always—and set the shower to a nice comfortable temperature.

Warm showers, one of the few creature comforts he lets himself enjoy.

When he towels off, his phone buzzes. He throws the towel over his shoulder, and peers at the screen. **Sorry, can't. Family dinner. Wish you could come.**

Nik sets the phone down and finishes drying off, before picking up his phone again to respond. There is another message waiting for him: **I'll call you when I'm home, okay?**

Nik smiles into his locker, as he types out a response. **Can't wait to hear your voice.**

Three dots appear immediately, so he keeps the screen lit while getting dressed. His eyes barely ever move away. When he emerges from his shirt neck, it simply says, **Me neither, guapo,** but Nik is grinning when he collects his things, and heads for the door.

"What are you all smiley about?" Percy asks, when they meet at the exit, and head out into the sunshine.

"Vasco texted."

Percy bumps into his side, "Are you seeing him tonight?"

Nik shakes his head, and wonders how much he should tell her. "This is weird," he says instead.

"Yeah," Percy agrees. "But it feels right, doesn't it?"

"Do you think we can be friends? After all this, you know?"

Percy hesitates for a moment, but when she speaks, her voice is confident. "I think so. I mean," she throws him an uncertain look, "we've essentially been roommates with benefits for a few years."

"More like the last decade," he grunts. "But yeah, I see your point."

She smiles at him encouragingly. "You can still tell me things, Nik."

"Things went well last night," he admits, his gaze determinedly on the ground in front of them. "I mean, everything is totally strange, and it feels like we are doing everything in the wrong order, but it was good."

He can feel her look at him, but doesn't meet her eyes. "Do you like him?"

Nik rubs a hand over his hair. "Yeah," he says finally. In his peripheral vision, he sees her cheeks round with a smile.

"Was it bad? Telling him about the situation, and asking him to keep things secret, and all that, I mean."

His eyes snap to her for a moment, and he sees the worry in her face, before looking away again.

"He was great about it, but it was—I don't know. Weird? Hard? Fuck, it was super weird. Weird and hard."

"Do you think Isavella would really go out with me?" Percy asks, when they reach the crosswalk by their house. He pushes the button, and answers, "She's been trying not to hit on you since we first became members there."

Percy scrunches up her face, and he has to drag her a little, when the light turns to *Walk*. "I'm not even sure I'm into women."

"Only one way to find out," Nik says while fumbling in his pocket for his house keys.

Percy leans her forehead against the door, so he doesn't turn the key. "What if she tells someone?"

Nik pulls her gently from the door, and unlocks it. He leads her inside, and tries to make his certainty shine through, when he tells her, that he is absolutely one hundred percent sure that Isavella will never do anything that could harm Percy.

In the end, Percy texts Isavella. She squeals like a school kid, as her thumb hovers over the button. He chuckles, and is suddenly certain that they can do this. Maybe they won't be able to save the Arctic, but they can definitely figure out the rest.

Thanks, pendejo

Vasco's finger hovers over the mouse button for a moment, before he submits his papers. Some part of him is convinced that his professors will be able to read the tremendous amounts of cannabis and coffee that have kept him going for the past six hours.

But with one presentation and three papers done, he feels justified to call it a day. One of them isn't even due until next week! He warms up some leftovers from the day before, and texts Jesus, Chippy, and Diego: **Rematch?**

He has lost about every game they have played since they first started their semi-regular video/board game club, as Diego reminds him immediately: **Looking for another chance to lose?**

But they still accept his self-invitation, and he is on his way over to their apartment five minutes later, a bag of tortilla chips under one arm, and a jar of salsa in the other.

He takes the elevator to the seventh floor, and walks down a hallway that smells of *yum yums* and microwave burritos. A door half-way down is ajar, and he catches a glimpse of two girls and a guy making out on a grimy couch, before another person shuts the door. He's not sure if he should think, *Good for them,* or warn them about STDs. He shakes his head, glad for the millionth time that he chose not to move into student housing.

A pair of eyes vanishes inside a dark room labeled "Do not enter," and he chuckles at the cliche-ness of it all. When he reaches the end of the hall, Diego opens the door after half a knock, and lets him in. Jesus and Gippy are in their usual positions already: Jesus upside down on the couch with his head hanging off, and Gippy lounged in a beanbag.

Jesus folds himself, and turns to roll off the couch. He slaps a palm onto Vasco's shoulder, and bumps his fist. Gippy lifts his head, opens one eye, and waves lazily in Vasco's general direction.

"Hangover?" he asks, with a gesture at his friend.

"Might actually be able to not be last today, cuate," Jesus laughs, and throws himself back onto the couch. Diego digs out the board games, holding a few up for votes, until they decide on a simple game of *Uno*.

Jesus unceremoniously dumps the chips into a bowl, and Gippy's hands are in the bowl before the salsa is even opened. He might not even remotely be Latinx like the rest of them, but they are clearly rubbing off. Soon, Gippy will have soaked up the entire Spanish language by osmosis—well, at the very least the insults and cuisine. They sit around the cracked tile table, and Jesus deals.

Diego pulls out his phone, and a moment later, music that throws Vasco back to his early video game days and late-night *Toni Hawks Pro Skater* begins to play, slightly tinny on the shitty speaker they bought for Jesus's birthday a few years back.

Ah, the joys of student life, Vasco thinks, and his thoughts drift to the stack of records in his room, Nik rifling through them, picking up a few.

Gippy's sudden "Earth to Vasco," pulls him back to the present, and he realizes it is his turn. He fans out his cards, and finds a yellow four to place on the green card in the middle of the table.

When Jesus threatens to get out the cone of shame—an accessory originally from the *Exploding Kittens* universe that very predictably made it into all of their games, including some that didn't even have turns—a few rounds later, Vasco forcefully pushes Nik from his thoughts yet again, and places another card on the pile.

Two hours later, Gippy throws his hand onto the table, and points a finger at Vasco. "I thought I could rely on you to lose, pendejo."

He holds up a finger, and discards his own hand.

"If you win the moment you are too distracted to focus, it's not the best sign," Diego deadpans, collecting all the cards and stacking them back into the box.

"Cerveca?" Jesus asks. Gippy and Diego nod enthusiatically.

"Just one," Vasco announces, "Family dinner tonight, so I can't stay long."

Jesus bends down to grab bottles from the fridge and hands them out. Diego grabs two of them, opens one with the other, before handing the closed one to Vasco.

"Thanks, pendejo," he laughs, as he searches for his keys and the attached bottle opener. He opens his, and hands the opener to Jesus.

"Salud!" they cheer, as they clink bottles. Vasco sets a timer on his phone, before allowing himself a second sip. Missing family dinner won't do.

When his alarm goes off, he peels himself off the couch, drops his empty bottle into the crate next to the fridge, and heads for the door. "Later, amigos."

The hallway is packed on his way out, and Vasco wonders if there is some kind of hall party scheduled for later. He wouldn't know, because his friends know better than to invite him to the lower end of student life at the dorms. He sidesteps a bulky football-type kid with a girl on his shoulders, almost steps into a puddle of who-knows-what, and breathes as shallowly as possible until he pushes through the building doors into LA's usual 72-degrees-and-sunny weather.

After the cave-like apartment Jesus, Diego, and Gippy share, his eyes water at the brightness, and he can't help but grin.

He's half-way to the subway, when his phone buzzes with a check-in from Ella who is making sure the entire family will be there for Sunday night dinner.

Wouldn't miss it for the world, he texts back, and leans against a pillar to wait for the next train.

Welcome to the chaos

"Gi, get the tamales from the counter, please," his mama yells over her shoulder, before she hugs him hello. "Hello, dear."

He kisses her cheek. "Hi, mama."

Giàu rushes past him, a tamales-laden tray balanced on top of a stack of dinner plates. She smiles at him, but her eyes never leave the plates.

Dee almost crashes into her when she takes the last few steps down in one go, and her socks slide on the tiles a little. The stack of plates wobbles noisily, before Dee's hands are there to steady them. Dee takes them out of Gi's hands, and Gi looks relieved.

"Welcome to the chaos," she dimples at him, and he puts an arm around her, as they walk into the dining room. Despite leaving on time, he is a few minutes late, but from the look of things, his trains are not the only ones running behind schedule.

His mothers are handing out plates and cutlery to their children, half of which are still standing around the table, rather than sitting down. They refuse his offers of help, so he sits in his usual chair, and lets Gi ladle soup into his bowl.

As always, dinner is a hodgepodge of cuisines. His mothers have taken fusion to a whole new level. By trying to include the cuisines of all their children's heritages, they added dishes from Ethiopia, Vietnam, India, Mexico, and Philadelphia—though they have been unable to import much more than vegan Philly Cheese "Steak" subs from the latter. By now, a lot of the dishes are so merged that no one can really tell what things once used to be.

The soup burns his tongue the tiniest bit, when he tries it, and he fans his mouth.

"You deserve that," his mom scolds, but she hands over the water pitcher nonetheless.

The tingling on his tongue is fading, when everyone is finally seated and served. He waits an extra few seconds while maintaining fierce eye contact with his mom, before digging in. She grins at him widely and mouths "Good boy!" before starting her own soup.

The soup has cooled enough to eat, and he tries another spoonful. "This is delicious," he exclaims, pointing at the soup with his spoon.

"Gi made it," his mama explains. "Mexican corn dumplings, honey?" She turns to face Giàu who nods.

"I found the recipe online," Giàu says, as if to make sure no one would give her credit.

"*You* made it perfectly, hon," their mama insists, and dips her spoon passionately into her own bowl.

Vasco eats and a fuzzy warmth fills his stomach and tugs at his heavy eyelids. When he finishes his soup, he stacks his bowl into Ella's. She passes it on, until a stack of seven arrives back in front of him. He gets up to carry them to the kitchen, but is surprised to find Ella at his side.

She follows him into the kitchen under the pretense of getting more beverages, but he's not fooled. Predictably, her elbow nudges his side the moment he sets down the plates. "How did it go?"

He swears to himself for the seven millionth time that he will never let her drag anything out of him ever again, and presses his mouth shut. She raises an eyebrow and smiles innocently, and it is all he needs to spill the beans. "Fine, I'll tell you. Stop looking at me like that."

She laughs. "That was too easy—even for you."

Okay, maybe he really wants to tell someone. Maybe, he's feeling like he'll explode if he holds his tongue for even one second longer. "I should never have told you," he says, but he doesn't even let her open her mouth to push him, before he's talking.

He tells her about how Nik stood in front of his door looking all strong and broody, about the tacos, about their walk. When she hugs him happily, he even tells her about their first kiss.

"Aww, Vasco!" she squeals, and he immediately regrets telling her anything. Except, he doesn't regret a thing, and if he's being totally honest, he feels like squealing along with her.

"When do I get to meet him?" she asks, and her feet are actually bouncing up and down.

"You have already met him!" he says, while pressing his hands onto her shoulders, to slow her bobbing.

She forces her feet to still, and looks at him, all trace of childishness gone. "Seriously, I can't wait to meet him."

"It's complicated," he grunts.

Ella's eyes soften, and a small smile tugs on her lips. "It always is. You don't need to date the husband of the richest woman in the state for things to get complicated."

He shushes her, looks over his shoulder. "Will you at least try to keep your voice down?"

So, she had put together who Nik was. He should've known she would. After meeting him at the bar, all she needed was to spot him with his wife, and put two and two together. "You know you can't tell anyone, right?" he whispers.

"What are you being all secretive about?" their mom asks, as she walks into the kitchen. "And where are those beverages you promised a decade ago, Ella?"

She grins at their caught-in-the-act expressions, winks, and turns to grab soda and beer from the fridge. She hands a few to each of them, and they follow her out of the kitchen, exchanging a last glance behind her back. Her "I've got you" look is all he needs to stop worrying, and he is grinning broadly when he sits back down at the table and listens to the six women in his life talk about their week.

They each talk about the good, the bad, the ugly, and the funny, but also about the little things, and Vasco feels the exhaustion seep through the contentment. Even the grin that won't leave his face can't keep him awake much longer. He eats too many tamales, clinks bottles with his mothers, Dee, and Ella. Gigi steals sips from Ella's bottle when their mothers are looking the other way, and Jo starts giggling uncontrollably when they almost get caught by their mom.

"Christmas isn't for another few months, girls—and Vasco—ah, shit, you know what I mean." They all laugh, and Vasco interjects, "Too used to finally being shot of me?"

"Took you long enough," Dee grins from the other end of the table.

"Better late than never," their mama says, but her wife is already talking again.

"You're all secretive and weird today, and I don't like it." It feels like a reprimand, but she's smiling. "If you're gonna let Jo drink behind my back, at least be better at hiding it."

They burst out laughing, and Jo blushes guiltily despite her complete sobriety—well, today. Vasco assumes she's not drinking for the same reason that she is in her wheelchair again: a fatigue that she can't hide completely. When she's not laughing, her eyelids droop, and he catches a few of the dog-like head shakes he has learned to interpret as Jo-Level-3 of exhaustion.

While his sisters explain that they are obviously very good at hiding it if their mama mixes up her daughters, he leans over to her. "You okay?"

She nods, but her laughter falters a bit. "Rough night."

He places a palm on her shoulder. "I know the feeling."

They both know it's not the same. No matter how sleepless his night has been, he'll never really understand what life is like for her.

Though, on days like today, after an all-nighter, too much caffeine, and a good meal, he feels closer to understanding what she's going through.

"I'm sorry you're not feeling well," he says, even though he's said it a thousand times before. "Do you want help getting upstairs?"

She nods, but then adds, "Not yet, though."

He rubs his palm over her back. "Let me know when you're ready."

She gives him a thankful smile, before jumping back into the conversation at the table, as if she never missed a beat. "She's basically 21, mom."

Vasco sits back and tries to catch up to the turns of the conversation. He knows there no such thing as multi-tasking, but Jo is impressively good at whatever people do instead. When he points this out to her a few minutes later, she chuckles. "Ten months on the kid's ward of a hospital, baby."

She makes it sound like she went to summer camp instead of spending almost a year at a children's hospital in Philadelphia getting ignored by doctor after doctor until Anna and Susan Cohen heard about her from a friend in the city, and flew out there to make them listen. Nothing like the joint forces of his parents to make people do their jobs. Another three months later, they brought her home, the latest addition to the Cohen family clan.

He grimaces helplessly, but she's already back to the conversation at large, and doesn't even see him.

Instead of trying to jump in, as well, he stacks more tamales onto his plate.

"Take some salad, sweetie," his mama says and hands over the bowl.

Obediently, he adds salad to his plate, and digs in. The conversation ebbs and flows through the tamales, and Vasco has to fight his exhaustion. When his mom offers up ice cream, he holds up his hands. "None for me, thanks. I really need to get home."

"The beloved 8 am class," Ella laughs, and he nods.

"And I won't have you there to make me breakfast," he smiles, as he pulls himself up. "Thank you for dinner, guys," he adds, as he walks around the table for hugs. He kisses his mom and his mama on their cheeks, before carrying his dirty dishes to the kitchen.

He catches Jo's eye, but she shakes her head and jerks it toward Ella. "Can't miss ice cream," she announces, then lowers her voice. "Thank you!" They smile at each other, before he turns and walks out of his childhood house. His phone is in his hand before he even reaches the curb. **Heading home now. Call you soon?**

The response is immediate, **I'll wait for you.**

He smiles, slides his phone into his pocket, and heads for the train station. Half an hour later, he's pushing through the turnstile at his home station.

You have an apology problem, babe

Nik shifts his phone from hand to hand, from surface to surface, as he keeps it close by. Percy is threatening to nail it to his forehead, when the screen finally lights up, and Vasco's name appears on the display.

"Good night," Percy calls over from the couch, when he rushes past toward his room.

"Night," he calls back, as he closes the door behind himself. He slides the button over. "Hey," he says when the call connects.

"Hey," Vasco's rough voice sounds over the line, and it is enough to make a grin split his face.

"Hey," he says again. "How was dinner at your family's?"

A car horn blares on Vasco's side. "Are you outside?" he asks without giving Vasco a chance to answer the first question.

"I'll be home in three minutes. I can call you then," Vasco says uncertainly, half-shouting over traffic noises around him.

"No, no, it's okay," Nik answers. "Couldn't wait?"

He half-regrets saying it, and his stomach plummets. Vasco laughs, and says, "I miss you." Nik almost chokes on the laugh that lifts the weight from his stomach which now seems to float underneath his lungs, pushing against his heart. And yes, he knows that none of this makes any anatomical sense.

A beeping makes Nik jump, and he almost drops his phone. "Hold on," Vasco says, and rustling tells Nik that he's lowered the phone. A moment later, the beeping stops, and Vasco's voice is back. "Sorry, stupid alarm. It seems to have imprinted on me like a baby duck or something. Only goes off when *I* enter."

"Sounds rough," Nik laughs, and settles in his reading chair. Marvin curls up next to the chair, as always ending up with his head at exactly the right spot for pets. Nik wonders again who is training whom in this relationship.

A moment of silence spreads, and Nik is weighing dozens of options for what to say, when Vasco breaks it. "I want to see you."

Nik's eyes flit up to the clock on his wall automatically. 9:45 pm. "I can be there in fifteen."

Vasco barks out a laugh. "I really need to sleep tonight."

Nik is out of his chair when he remembers that he has to attend a board meeting the next morning. "And I have an early meeting," he groans. "Fuck, I miss you."

He slumps back into the chair, and resumes his petting of Marvin's head. Marvin looks up at him, one eye open, before lowering his head to the bed, and resuming his 17-hours-a-day nap.

"I have an idea," Vasco says after a moment. "You said that you didn't want to skip steps. You wanted to go through the motions or whatever."

Nik blushes, but bites his tongue.

"Have you ever heard about *Janosch's Traumstunde*?" Nik doesn't understand the last words, so he admits, "Since I am not even sure what language you just spoke, I guess not."

"*Janosch's Traumstunde*," Vasco repeats more slowly, but it's no help to Nik who is still completely lost. Though he thinks the language is European. "It's German. Well, Traumstunde is. Janosch is a name. Anyway, the guy wrote this kid's story about a tiger and a bear—I think it was a bear. I don't know. Some kind of animal—anyway. They don't like their home, and then something arrives (was it a banana crate?) and it says 'Panama' on there, and the bear, or the tiger, or whatever, convinces the other one to go to Panama. He describes it as this great adventure thing, though he only knows the name. Well, they set out for Panama, and travel for a while. After quite some time, they get back to where they started. Their house is overgrown, and the old crate—yeah, I think it was a crate—has fallen apart, so that it looks like a sign that says 'Panama.' They think they've made it. They don't recognize their home, but because they think it's something else, they love it."

Nik rubs his chin. "I'm not sure where you are going with this, and I have a million questions, but go on."

"I swear there was a point to this story, though I'm not quite sure how I was going to tie the bow. Ah, yeah, something like this: it's not about the labels we apply to things. It doesn't matter if they got to Panama or if they just found their Panama. So, we can't go on a fucking date at a restaurant. But, we can have our own date."

"Still not following fully, but I'm listening. But don't think you'll get out of telling me why you know German kid's stories."

Vasco laughs, and Nik's heart beats a little faster.

"My mama is German," Vasco says as an aside, before returning to his previous topic. "What are dates about?" Nik hesitates, but Vasco isn't waiting for an answer. "If you think about it, dates are about getting to know the other person in a safe way. As you spent the night—well, most of it—at my place, I'm pretty sure safety isn't why you want to go on a date."

"Fuck, I hadn't even thought of safety. Thinking about safety and first-date rules makes it even worse that I essentially pressured you into meeting at your place. I'm sorry."

Vasco's voice is firm, when he says, "Don't apologize for what happened yesterday. Please, Nik, don't."

"I'm sorry," Nik says again, though he's apologizing for an apology now, and he's just digging himself deeper.

Vasco laughs, rough and low, "You have an apology problem, babe."

Nik's heart flutters, and his cheeks heat. "So-sorry?" he asks through a wide grin.

They both laugh, and Vasco wheezes a little as he fights for breath.

"Anyway," Vasco says when they have calmed down enough to continue the conversation. "If you strip first dates down to their essence, it's about getting to know people. And we can do that. We don't have to skip the steps. We just have to alter them. Don't ask me how it all connects to Janosch, though."

But Nik's got the message. It doesn't matter if the Panama story made sense. It doesn't matter how it all fits together, because it somehow does. What matters much more is that Vasco is trying, and that is what makes Nik's heart summersault around his chest.

"Thank you," he says gently, and Vasco's voice softens in response. "I guess it's time for our first date then."

"Wasn't that yesterday?" Nik asks, remembering Vasco's lips on his, his back against the wall, and panting breaths.

Vasco clears his throat and Nik is certain he's remembering, too. "I was going to declare yesterday some kind of setting-out-the-rules night, but you've got a point. Would you like to go on a second first date?"

Nik laughs, his mind still occupied with the remnants of memory. "Yes, I'd like that."

"How about we get some actual sleep tonight, and I take you on a date—at my place—tomorrow?"

"I would like that very much." Nik sits on his blanket, and pulls his pillow from its shelf. He slips underneath the blanket, and scoots his back against the wall.

"Are you in bed?" Vasco asks, and Nik mhh-mhhs a confirmation. Nik yawns and doesn't succeed at suppressing the sound.

"Good night, guapo" Vasco whispers. "I can't wait to see you tomorrow."

Nik's lip curls into a smile. He loves it when Vasco calls him babe, but when he calls him guapo, his entire body responds—a warm, fuzzy buzz that makes him feel floaty. He knows that their first date isn't until tomorrow, but there's nothing first-date about the way he fells about Vasco.

White, sixties, blue suit

Nik is in the most boring meeting the world has ever held. Or at least he thinks so. Not that he's been in a lot of meetings. He's wearing a suit and fucking dress shoes. Percy even knotted a god-forsaken tie around his neck. He feels as if he might suffocate—all over his body.

He's never felt as out of place as in this meeting. The fact that Reginald fucking Bold is here doesn't help. The man has a monocle, for Christ's sake. But while his name might be on the door of the building, he's no longer in any capacity at the firm. Silent investors shouldn't be yapping around a board room about quarterly returns and excel spreadsheets or whatever it was that these people actually talked about.

He closes his eyes and takes a deep breath. He wonders how long it has been since he has last checked the time, but he has a feeling it hasn't been long enough. Is that stupid thing even working? There's no way he's only been here for an hour.

He tries to listen to the tiny Big man for a while but he can't find the ends of sentences—or figure out the beginnings, and he is lost. He finds his thoughts drift to the uneven wig line of the balding business man in a corner—again!—and bites his tongue. He can't look bored. Percy needs him looking as if he knows what's going on. And he *has* studied this shit. Well, not the math-and-spreadsheets shit, but the environmental shit.

Percy's hand squeezes his thigh, and he looks at her briefly. Her reassuring smile confirms he's not looking as relaxed as he would like to. Damn it.

Okay, Nikau, you got this.

Reginald Bold sits down in his seat, and the actual chairman takes over. The slimy bastard thanks Mr. Bold, before addressing the agenda: The Arctic Project. Finally, something remotely interesting, so there's a lot less risk of drooling all over his empty notepad.

"As you know," the chair man—white, sixties, blue suit—explains, "we've been talking about project White Bear for a while now." White Bear. Even the code name is lunacy. "It's time to talk shop. I've asked Percy here to run the models for us, and she tells me, she's ready. I guess, we'll find out." He chuckles, and the room chuckles with him.

Nik catches his upper lip before it turns up in a growl. The way the chairman talks about Percy makes him fiercely protective of his wife. No, of his ex-wife. No, his friend. Ah, crap. Nevermind. And even if she wasn't his wife, or his friend, or whatever, no one should be talked to like that.

"Of course, Mr. Chairman, sir," Percy says politely, as she rises from her chair. He scoots toward the table a little to let her through, and watches, as she takes her spot at the podium. She's in a burgundy skirt that ends just above her knees, and a glossy gray blouse. Her hair is up in a bun so tight Nik is sure it hurts.

A man—white, sixties, gray suit—holds up his pen, and the chairman addresses him immediately, "Yes, Mr. Wagner?"

Misogynistic prick.

The gray suit answers, "Thank you, Mr. Chairman. It's nothing urgent really." Nik barely suppresses an eye roll. "But I'd like to mention that the general public doesn't seem to look too kindly on the Arctic project. Has Persephone taken that into account?"

Nik turns to Percy. She looks calm and composed, but he can tell she is agitated by the way her shoulders are just a little further back than usual and the tilt of her head. Their eyes meet and he tilts up one side of his mouth. She blinks at him once, both eyes closing for just a moment longer, before she returns her attention to the gray suit and the chairman.

Nik has lost track of the conversation, but it doesn't seem to matter, because Percy's got it. "I'm sorry, Mr. Wagner, but may I suggest you let me present, before asking questions. You see, sir, I have added a table of contents to the second slide, and you'll be able to get an idea of the topics I have taken into account."

The man mumbles something, but shuts up and leans back in his chair. A few clicks later, Percy has pulled up a presentation on the wall behind her, and Nik tries to listen, but even though it is the Arctic project, and even though it is Percy talking, he just can't follow any of the math or the business kauderwelch.

Nik's right butt cheek is falling asleep by the time Percy is done presenting. When the men around the table are done asking questions, the other side has followed, and he's wobbling around in his chair as inconspicuously as he can manage to wake up his ass.

Percy hands over the podium to the next speaker—white, sixties, blue suit— and sits down next to Nik. She squeezes his knee for a moment, before returning her fingers to her keyboard.

Two more speakers follow this one—white, sixties, more boring suits—and Nik is convinced his ass will fall off or whatever the equivalent of losing a foot is. He raises his hand with Percy every time someone calls for a vote, and otherwise sits in his chair, trying not to ponder how long it takes to permanently damage blood vessels from restricted blood flow. And why the fuck would anyone design meeting room chairs this uncomfortable?

Finally the chairman declares the meeting over, and the first people stuff laptops under arms, papers into briefcases. He clenches his hands until at least half of the men around the table have risen. He gets up and shakes out his legs, trying to wake up his ass without looking like a complete lunatic.

Percy leads him through a maze of hallways with an odd elegance despite the hospital-ward-meets-art-gallery style. They reach her office, and her hand on his back guides him inside. She closes the door, and turns to face him. He scans the room which would look at home in any of the many lawyer TV shows he has seen, and once he's made sure no one will judge him, begins to hop around, bends down by the waist. Percy chuckles, and when he re-emerges from his impromtu yoga-dance hybrid, he finds her face red from suppressed laughter.

"You okay?" she splutters.

He nods and gestures at himself. Percy has witnessed his body falling asleep many times, so he's not surprised when she doesn't ask any questions. "How do you stand these things?" he asks through his teeth.

She shrugs. "I can't wait to get rid of them. Nothing more annoying than buttering up to a bunch of Caucasian grandpas with god complexes."

"Who think women are worth nothing at all," he interjects.

"This would be a lot easier if I'd been born the son my father wanted," Percy sighs, but her smile returns quickly. "Thank you for not killing any of those assholes."

He laughs. "Wasn't easy."

If he's being honest, he still doesn't even understand why exactly he is at the meetings. Percy had assigned him a board seat after inheriting her shares, but Nik knows way too little about big corporations to understand the dynamics.

"Ready to go home?" Percy asks. He nods, though he can't help thinking that it hasn't been home in a long time.

Go with the flow?

"If you're going to have a real first date tonight, you should do it here," Percy suggest, as she unlocks the door.

"That would be weird," Nik states, and doesn't even fully explore the idea. He loosens the tie around his neck more than he did the moment they were in the car, and opens a few buttons on the dress shirt.

"I won't be here," she says, as she hangs up her purse.

He feels his face split into a grin. "Are you meeting Isavella?"

Percy blushes, tiny splotches of color on her cheeks, and admits, "Yes, I'm going to talk to her tonight. She doesn't know it's a date yet. I might chicken out."

He grabs her by the shoulders, and lowers his head a little. "No, you won't. You'll follow your heart and not your brain, and finally let someone love you the way you deserve to be loved."

She leans her forehead against his chest, his arms a buffer between them. She tenses, squeals, and does a tiny tap dance of frustration. He pushes her back gently to make her face him. "You deserve to be with someone who makes you light," he echoes her words.

"You don't know she loves me," she insists.

"Of course, I don't," he says in a calm tone. "But it's worth trying."

"I don't even know if I'm in love with her," she argues.

"Of course, you are." He places a hand on her cheek. "You know. Just look at yourself. You were never like this when we met."

She leans into the touch. "I thought I was in love with you."

"Me too, Cheeks. Me too."

They stand in the hallway for a moment, before Percy breaks the touch, and sits down to take off her shoes. She places them neatly underneath the bench, and he doesn't even comment on the change in habit. He's very proud of himself for not teasing her about it.

A little too proud probably.

"So, as I was saying," she says, and he leans his shoulder against the hallway wall. "You should meet here. Get some food delivered from *Quo Vadis* and enjoy the evening."

Nik pauses to consider the option, but Percy isn't done talking. "You could use the rooftop jacuzzi."

And with that comment, Nik is no longer wondering if it is weird to invite your date to your wife's house—*I mean, fuck it, everything is weird!*—and instead adds a mental note to research some constellations to impress Vasco with.

Percy grins, and she knows she's done it. Nik is sure of it. Water, warmth, open skies—the perfect combination to pull him out of any self-imposed shell.

"I'm leaving in half an hour. I'm meeting Isavella for a workout first."

Nik checks the time on his phone. 5:45 pm. Okay, if he's gonna do this, it's time to get started. He texts Vasco, **Would it be too strange to meet at my place? You haven't prepped anything, right? I can have you picked up at your place. I know you don't have a car. Does 7 work for you? Do you like Italian food? Any allergies? Can you bring swim shorts?**

He presses send, then realizes he's asked a million questions, and starts typing an apology, before he remembers Vasco's words. *You have an apology problem.* So, instead, he sets his phone down, and finds Percy still next to him. She looks at him with a face that tells him, he's ignored her.

"Sorry, did you say something?"

She smiles. "That's new. You admitting you weren't listening."

He scoffs in mock-outrage. "I am *always* listening."

His phone buzzes, and his gaze jumps to the screen. He hears Percy's giggle, but has thoughts only for the message on the screen. **7 works. No allergies. Many questions.**

He looks up, Percy's patience somehow still not ending. They both laugh, and she repeats what she said. "Do you want me to call *Quo Vadis* for you?"

He really, really does, but it feels cowardly to admit it. He shakes his head, but her gaze softens further, and when she adds, "I know how much you hate phone calls, Nik. I really don't mind," he caves.

"Thank you, Percy."

She walks over to the drawer by the fridge and digs out a business card. No, not a menu like normal people. A velvety business card. And there's no sign of red, green, and white or any other variation of cliche Italy flair. Sturdy white paper, gold letters.

"What do you want?" she asks, but then she waves him off. "Never mind, I've got it."

She dials the number on her phone, and he loiters nearby as she orders an assortment of numbers and dishes. Looks like their dinner will be a surprise for both of them.

"Serving ware, please, Giovanni," Percy adds, and Nik chuckles at the reminder that there is one final cliche left about the place. "Thank you, you are amazing. Mille grazie."

She mutes her phone. "7.30?"

He nods, and she unmutes her phone to finish the conversation. He hugs her, brief and tight, and thanks her again. "I don't know what I'd do without you," he says, and immediately corrects himself. "I don't know what I will do without you."

She palms his shoulder, and smiles. "Just because we didn't work out as a couple doesn't mean we have to leave each other's lives. I won't be able to order your dinners for you, but I'll be there if you need me."

He wonders how many more grown-up conversations he'll have to survive in the next months, and decides to hug her again instead of figuring out how to make words work. He puts everything he wants to say into the hug and it is in that moment that he knows things will be okay. The energy between them has changed. There is no spark, no attraction. And while there is still love, Nik knows better now than to read it as romance.

Very suddenly, she is letting go of him, twirling on the spot to check her phone. "Damn it, I need to get ready."

And before he can utter even a single word, she dashes out of the kitchen and toward her room, only to reemerge ten seconds later with her gym bag in one hand, clothes in the other. She dumps the bag next to the door, one-eighties, and heads for the bathroom. Ten minutes later, she has rushed enough to leave her with time to spare.

Nik indulges her small talk, because she looks too nervous to leave to her own devices, but he is glad when she finally announces it is time to leave. Nik has a feeling she'll be super early anyway, but Isavella won't mind.

"I'll text you a heads-up when I know I'll be home. But don't worry, I won't be home anytime before 11."

"Do you want Vasco out of here when you get home?" he asks, suddenly very aware of the potential for a meeting between them.

"I would love to meet him, but you'll have to decide if it's weird. Just go with the flow, Nik."

"Go with the flow?" he grins.

"I don't know. You know what I mean. I was going to go for 'read the room,' but we both know how excellent you are at that."

He doesn't take offense. No one should get offended by facts. And he definitely, absolutely, is shit at reading a room.

"Changing the wording doesn't really change the idea." He waves a hand around. "But, yes, I'll figure it out."

She bobs her head once and rushes out of the door without another word. Nik stands rooted to the spot until the door hits the frame and pulls him from his thoughts. He doesn't have much time left, so he heads to his room and takes off what he thinks of as his business-man costume. He hangs the suit onto the wardrobe door in Percy's room—after hovering outside it for an awkward moment, before firmly telling himself that it's no big deal and that it is where his suit has always been, where he picked it out this morning.

He showers off the day with his hair up in a bun to keep it dry, and is impressed with himself when it only takes two attempts to pick an outfit, though it's probably not too impressive considering he owns a very minimal wardrobe.

He opens the door and accepts a very happy Marvin back from the dog walker, again wondering why she's called a dog walker when she is essentially a babysitter for dogs and does so much more than just walk them. "I cleaned him at the dog park, and walked him here from my house, so he's had a chance to dry off. He should be all dry, but fair warning, just in case."

He thanks her, pats Marvin's head which is just the tiniest bit damp, so the hair sticks to his palm, and closes the door behind her.

"You smell like dog," he tells Marvin, who looks at him guiltily.

So, hybrid first-second date?

The driver pulls up, and Vasco steps out of the black limousine, and Nik lets him in. Vasco is in a crinkled, washed-out red button-down that somehow looks on purpose, and a pair of dark-blue denims. Marvin whines on his bed, but Nik can't stop looking at Vasco, who smiles an open-mouthed smile that Nik wants to kiss off his face.

"Hey," he manages, and Vasco returns, "Hola, guapo."

A shiver runs down Nik's spine at the words, and he wonders if Vasco knows how much he likes it. Vasco holds up a a pair of aquamarine swim shorts with blue stripes, and raises an eyebrow.

"Dinner will be here soon," Nik says instead of answering the implied question.

Vasco chuckles, and places the swim wear on the hallway bench. He takes off his shoes, and tucks them in between the pairs underneath. Nik watches and smiles to himself.

Vasco gets up and walks straight up to Nik, grabbing him around the waist with an arm. "I know this is supposed to be our first date, but—" He kisses Nik, slowly, and Nik melts. He closes his eyes, and lets himself fall into the kiss, explores the taste of the first man he has ever kissed. Vasco's arm is strong around him, and he slides a hand up Vasco's back, rests the other on his chest. He inhales Vasco's scent, and looses himself in the moment.

When they break apart, Nik rests his forehead against Vasco's and keeps his eyes shut. "But?" he whispers.

"Hm?"

Nik chuckles softly. "You said this was our first date, but..."

Vasco releases a soft laugh, almost a whisper. "No need to take steps backward, is there?"

"So, hybrid first-second date?" Nik draws back, and takes Vasco's head into his palms. He strokes a strand of hair from his face, and places a peck on his temple.

Vasco covers Nik's hand with his and answers, "Something like that."

A knock on the door behind them, makes them jump apart. They laugh, and Vasco presses a palm to his own mouth, retreating around a corner. Marvin paws the door, but sits when Nik reaches for the handle. "Good boy," Nik rewards him, then turns to the woman outside. "I apologize for making you wait. I didn't expect you until 7:30."

Even his complaints are apologies. Fuck, Vasco is right. He does indeed, very much, have an apology problem.

"I am very sorry, Mr. Miller," she says, and he decides not to correct the name. "May I set up?"

He nods, remembers Vasco hiding around the corner, and shakes his head. She looks at him in confusion. "Would you like me to return at the right time, sir?"

"No, no. That's okay. I'll take them. Don't worry about it."

He takes the heavy boxes from her hands, and there is a moment of hesitation where Nik isn't sure she will let go. He wonders if she worries about him returning the boxes—no, she wouldn't dare. Not after years of catering for the company and delivering to Percy and him.

"Really, I've got it. Everything is fine." He turns in a half circle for a moment, before setting the boxes down on the hallway bench. He reaches around the door for the bill Percy has attached to the magnet board there. "Here, for you. Thank you so much."

He closes the door despite her spluttering, picks up the boxes again, and sends Marvin to his bed. When he turns, Vasco is leaning against the wall, smooth as fuck. Nik wants to drop the boxes and kiss him all over again, but they are here to have dinner, and it won't do to serve it cold.

"Want any help?" Vasco asks, as he idles over, a hand resting on Nik's back. It feels right. Nik has no other word for it. The handsome guy who didn't judge his panic attack outside a fundraiser is in his kitchen, and there is nothing weird about it, nothing at all.

He hands over the boxes, and Vasco begins to set up on the dining table just outside the kitchen in the weird half-open kitchen/dining space that is somehow also the entrance hall, and a lounge area. Honestly, Nik will never understand rich people houses. "Real plates–no, formal serving ware? This isn't takeout."

Nik shrugs, as he removes a plastic lid from one of the serving trays. "The restaurant that does the catering for the highest of the higher ups at Percy's company does personal catering. Percy and I have been loyal customers for years. Well, we usually don't get the fancy plates."

Nik stacks the lids neatly next to the sink, so he can clean them before returning them to the restaurant. He grabs plates, cutlery, hands them to Vasco, before returning to the kitchen for drinks. "What do you want to drink?" He calls out to Vasco. "Water, beer, some weird fancy berry lemonade—don't ask me for details. Percy gets it from a small artisan store, and she brings a different one every time. I never know what they are until I try them. Okay, sometimes I still don't know after I try them. They are usually good though. It's Italian food– maybe you prefer wine? We have white, red, rose, probably even champagne, but that's not exactly Italian. Anyway, what would you like?"

He knows he's rambling, but for once he doesn't feel self-conscious about it. This is him, and the way Vasco makes him feel, also makes him bold enough to put little pieces of himself out there. When he looks at Vasco, Vasco is smiling, and Nik doesn't even wonder if he's making fun of him.

Vasco chooses beer with a request for the strange lemonade later, and Nik grabs two from the fridge. Beer, not lemonade.

"This smells delicious," Vasco comments, as he sits down across from Nik. "I don't know what half of these things are called."

Nik scans the table. He should've listened when Percy ordered. "Percy ordered, so I don't know what everything is, but those are some fancy version of pizza bites, marinated olives—careful, they are very garlicky!—tasting platter, and this is bruschetta."

"We'll figure out the rest, as we try it," Vasco says, and helps himself to bruschetta. He takes a bite and moans his appreciation, before continuing. "How are things between you?"

Nik takes a sip of his beer. "I thought it would be weird. It was at first, but we've been nothing more than friends with benefits for years." Vasco's hand pauses on the way to his mouth, tomato pieces tumbling onto his plate, so Nik presses on, "Going from there to friends without benefits was a lot easier than I thought. There were some awkward moments, especially in the first days, but then something shifted." Vasco takes a bite, and Nik relaxes a little. "It's as if we were never anything more."

Vasco sits back in his chair, and the silence between them stretches for a moment. "I need to ask you one thing. I promise I'll only ask it once. We can move on to first-date things right after. Is that okay?"

Nik's heart thumps, but he nods. "Of course, anything."

Vasco looks at Nik directly, and Nik makes sure to hold his gaze. "Do you still have feelings for your wife or any desire to get intimate with her?"

Without hesitation, he answers, "I love her as a friend, but I have no romantic feelings for her, and I don't desire her in any way."

Vasco nods, and somehow Nik knows he's said what Vasco needed to hear. "Okay," Vasco says, and finishes his bruschetta in one giant bite. "This is fucking delicious. Have you tried this?"

Nik barks a laugh, thankful for the change in topic. "Bruschetta is so high on the list of my favorite foods, that Percy made the restaurant add a gluten-free version."

"This is gluten-free?" Vasco asks in surprise, and grabs another slice. He nibbles off a bite without tomato, and mmhs. "Nope, this is good."

Nik dips his spoon into his minestrone, and blows the hot liquid. How is Vasco through two slices of bruschetta before he has taken even a first bite?

"So, tell me, Nik," Vasco says in a way that makes Nik think of a radio host, "what do you like to do?"

When Nik looks at him, and can't manage more than "Um, I, er, I like..."

"I'm kidding, babe," Vasco laughs. "I want to get to know you, but I don't think the 21-questions approach is exactly your style."

Nik laughs, and takes a large gulp of his beer. "You sound like you have a better plan."

Vasco's grin is mischievous, when he responds. "Is there anything in your phone's picture roll that you are embarrassed of?"

Nik's first instinct is panic, but when he thinks about his photos, he can't think of anything that he would mind sharing with Vasco. "No," he answers, but it comes out more as a question than a response.

"Good," Vasco grins, "then, yes, I do have an idea."

Nooooo, je ne regrette rien

They eat quickly, a few attempts at small talk, a few jokes, and while the food is delicious, Vasco can't wait to be done. Nik sits across from him, slowly warming up a little, and Vasco is tempted to go for another joke to break the last bit of the nervousness.

He half-regrets even asking about Persephone earlier, but he had to be sure.

When Vasco has tried every dish and eaten second helpings of his favorites, he stretches in his chair.

Nik takes a final biteful of—ah, he can't remember what it even was. Nevermind. Nik finishes his, er, food, and sets down his fork. "Finished?" he asks, and Vasco nods.

Nik gets up and carries plates and bowls into the kitchen. Vasco follows with his own stack. Nik opens a cupboard filled with matching glass containers, and picks out stretching lids for their leftovers. Somehow, the fact that they match—as opposed to the assortment of random jars from grocery foods in his own and his mothers' kitchens—drives home just how much more money Nik seems to have.

He's experienced moments like this one all night. The first when a black limousine picked him up at his house, and a cheerful driver named Mike asked about his music preferences. The second had been when he stepped into the apartment. It wasn't the magazine-cover interior design that got to him as much as the sheer amount of empty space available. But there had been more throughout the night: the 20-dollar tip Nik had handed the delivery person, the food selection that could feed his entire family of six, and now the fucking matching food containers.

Nik stacks the dishes next to the sink, and asks Vasco to place the leftovers into the fridge. When he opens the door, he can't manage to shut his face anymore. "Damn, even your fridge sparkles, man. How do you keep the place this... um... meticulous?"

Nik barks a laugh, and Vasco's insides feel like warm sunshine. "We have a cleaner who comes once every week, but I canceled on him this week."

"So, who cleaned all of this?"

The accomplished, and yet somehow embarrassed, look on Nik's face answers before he does. "I might have gone a little overboard with my mate consumption and gotten restless."

"It looks great." Vasco closes the fridge, and turns to Nik who is leaning Nik leans against the counter.

"So, I thought," Nik says, "we could go to the rooftop patio for the rest of the night."

"You've got a rooftop patio?" Vasco exclaims, and there's probably some jealousy in his voice.

Nik blushes. "Look, man, I really don't like living like this." He pushes off the counter, and grabs Vasco's hand. "Come, let me show you something."

Nik pulls Vasco along a hallway, past a bathroom with the door ajar enough to see a rimless bathtub and fluffy white towels, and into a room at the end of the hall. Nik's room. Nik's room which is nothing like the rest of the house. A low desk in one corner, an open wardrobe in another. The main piece of furniture seems to be a cozy reading chair with a fluffy blue foot rest and an e-reader on a thrifted-looking stool. Marvin is curled up in the chair—when did he stop hovering underneath the table hoping for scraps?—and snoring spectacularly. Plants cover the window sill and a small shelf. There are no golden picture frames with expensive art here, either. Three simple black frames above the reading chair are the only decorative items.

"The Little Prince," he asks after inspecting the first. The font on the cover reads *Le Petit Prince*, so Vasco adds, "In French?"

Nik looks at the picture as if he has forgotten it is there. "It's the only thing I have left of my grandmother. When I was younger, I used to read the book when I stayed at her house for the summer."

"You speak French?" Vasco asks, and Nik shrugs. "Not anymore. I learned it in school. Learned Spanish, too. But I forgot everything, and now all I can do is quote Moulin Rouge or Édith Piaf."

"Nooooo, je ne regrette rien," Vasco sings off-tune, and they both laugh. "Yeah, that's pretty much the extend of my French."

Vasco moves over to the second picture frame, an Aquarelle drawing of a bird with a long beak. "It's a kiwi," Nik explains.

"New Zealand, right?" Vasco asks.

Nik nods. "Yeah. Percy and I visited a few years back. We spent a month touring the islands in 2016. Did you know they are the birds with the shortest beaks?"

Vasco looks at the painting again. "Um? Doesn't look very short to me."

Nik points at the drawing. "See the nostrils? They are at the tip of the beak. And when whoever decided what a beak is, they set out the rule to measure from nostril to beak tip."

Vasco places an arm around Nik's hip and draws him closer. He nudges his head at the room. "Thank you."

Nik looks around his own room, as if he's never seen it before. "I don't like stuff."

"I wasn't judging you. You know that, right?"

Nik leans into him a little. "I still wanted you to know that that apartment out there isn't me. It's not Percy either, to be honest. We took a wrong turn somewhere and every time we realized we weren't happy, we upgraded something. It doesn't work."

Nik puts an arm around Vasco's shoulder, and guides him out of the room. He grabs a speaker from a side table by the stairs, and they head upstairs to a maisonette area with book shelves and bean bags.

"This looks comfortable. Do you read up here?"

Nik shakes his head. "I prefer my room."

Vasco understands it's not the room nor the chair.

Nik opens the patio door and Vasco follows him outside. His gaze is immediately drawn to the view on his right: the city lights glitter like colored stars over McMansions, huge tree crowns, and, though it can barely be seen, the ocean at the far horizon. "Wow."

He walks over to the railing and puts his hands on the metal. Nik walks up behind him, slides his hands over his, and kisses his cheek. "Good thing, narcissists like their privacy."

The view is blocked in three directions: a tall tree on one side, a wall behind them to what Vasco thinks must be the stairwell, and the house on their right. But even the view to the front is directional. All the mansions face the sunset with only tinted windows in the upper stories facing other mansions. God forbid someone might see a neighbor. Freaks.

He shakes his head, and feels Nik's laugh against his neck. "Does that mean, I get to do this?" he asks and pulls himself around to face Nik. He slides a hand over the man's cheek, traces the line of his jaw, and kisses him. Nik responds with strong, slow kisses, that make Vasco shiver. Shooting stars dance on his skin where Nik touches his neck, his shoulder.

They break apart, and neither of them speaks while they watch the sunset together. They stand at the railing, nosing each other, as the purple fades to indigo. Nik traces goosebumps on Vasco's arm, and leads him over to the hammock. Vasco sinks in and watches as Nik lights the fire—all show, not much warmth—and grabs a giant but thin blanket from a chest next to a *Weber* grill.

"Come here for a second," Nik requests and holds out a hand. When Vasco takes it, Nik pulls him up and into his arms and presses another brief kiss onto his mouth, before releasing him. He hooks two ropes into carabiners on the wall and pulls Vasco along with him into the hammock.

Their feet hang out on one side of the hammock, while their backs lean against the other. The ropes, Vasco understands, keep the hammock from closing in on itself. Images flash through his mind. Nik on top of him inside the hammock. Deep kisses, searching hands.

He pulls himself from his thoughts, and takes out his phone instead. He sets it to Do Not Disturb, and opens the gallery app.

He nestles against Nik, until they can both see his screen. Images zoom past, as he scrolls to the very top. He clicks on the first photo, the last remaining memory of an oak tree Dee and him drew onto the living room wall of their old house.

And suddenly, he is nervous. He closes his eyes for a moment, tightens his hold on Nik's arm around his hip, before he starts to speak.

I want to hear your version

Vasco's voice shakes a little, but gets steadier with every word. "We painted this for Ella when she turned 10."

"How old were you then," Nik asks.

"Twenty-two, I think," Vasco says, "She was having a tough time at school because a teacher said something thoughtless about Indians—her heritage. I told you all of us are adopted, right?"

Nik nods. "Your mothers said it in their speech." Percy had put two and two together for him the other day: the two women who talked about adopting children from all over the world while managing a kind of charity for charities Nik still has a lot of questions about. But they can wait.

"Oh, right. I forgot you heard the glorified version already."

There is disappointment in Vasco's voice, but also something a lot like resignation if Nik is interpreting it right. In moments like this one, he wishes he was better at reading other people's emotions.

"I want to hear your version," Nik says gently, and Vasco relaxes into him. He switches over to *Signal* and pulls up a group chat. He selects a photo from the media roll. "Ella," he introduces. "She's 21, I think." He hesitates, thinks for a moment. "Yeah, she's 21. My mothers adopted her when she was still a baby, just over a year old."

He switches back to the tree. "I was 13, knee deep into my ugliest teenage bullshit. Dee had just outgrown the worst, and I really didn't want another baby in the house, but Ella and I." He breathes out a laugh. "She loved me so much, she broke through my layers of rebellion. When mama couldn't get her to calm down, I could. But she didn't have it easy. I don't know why the kids at her school picked her." He scoffs. "That school was about 90 percent kids like us. What do the politicians call it? Kids with migration backgrounds? Whatever. But she was strong. She does her name justice. Ela." He draws the name out a little longer. "It means oak. When she got to the US, her birth certificate was soaked through, and her name was hard to make out. Could've been Ella or Ela. Ella seemed easier here in the US, so they went with that."

"Why couldn't she be with her family?"

Vasco's thump traces circles on Nik's wrist. "We don't know all the details. She got dropped off at the hospital in the middle of the night."

Vasco lifts up the screen a little. "That's why we painted the oak. We wanted her to know what she means to us. She's so fucking stable, it's unbelievable. And she's kinda the rock—or tree trunk, I guess—of the family."

He taps the photo, scrolls past a few, opens another. A photo of a much younger Vasco with paper glasses that look like the old 3D kind. "Cute," Nik comments.

"I went to see *Puss in Boots* with a few friends. I don't remember anything except for that image with the giant eyes that became a meme later."

The next photo shows a white hamster with dirt all over his fur, poking its adorable little head out of a hole. "Moby Dick. Dee rescued her from school after an idiot teacher used her for an experiment. And Dee got *really* obsessed. She went to the library and rented as many books on hamsters as she could carry."

The sky darkens and the first stars glow faintly. The light of the fire dances over Vasco's profile, and Nik's chest feels made of cotton candy: soft, fluffy, and about to melt into goo. He kisses Vacso's ear and holds him tight.

"She didn't rent a single book on keeping a hamster. All books about hamsters in their natural habitats. I think that hamster was the happiest hamster in captivity ever alive." Vasco is smiling nostalgically.

He tells Nik more about Dee, Lesedi, the oldest of his sisters, and the first to get adopted into the family after Vasco. "They never wanted to adopt more children. I was supposed to be enough." The same emotion Nik couldn't place earlier is lacing Vasco's words, and Nik thinks it might be a feeling he knows really well. "They adopted Dee when she was a newborn. One of the non-profits they worked with was called in to help with a massacre in Ethiopia. She was one of two to survive in her village."

Nik's throat feels tight, and Vasco's voice is raspy, so he gently pushes Vasco to his side, and grabs the fancy lemonades he'd offered Vasco before from the patio fridge. He opens the bottles with the opener on the wall, and hands one to Vasco. They cling bottles, but neither of them says a word until Nik is comfortable at Vasco's side.

"I was 11 when they adopted her, and she screemed so much. And then the annoying thing started talking at six months old. She never shut up again. Either she was crying her eyes out or she was babbling. I loved her, but I also hated her. But—" Vasco takes a sip. "I don't think any of it was about her." He turns his head to look at Nik. "I felt like my parents didn't think I was enough. I was jealous of how much attention they were giving her. Don't get me wrong: I love my sisters, all of them. But it hasn't always been easy."

Nik kisses Vasco's forehead. "I understand."

Vasco shows him images of family vacations that all seemed to be a day trip away from Los Angeles. He shows him images of pets they owned, videos of squirrels that stole nuts from their porch. He shares the demolition of the house with the oak tree, and tells Nik there were too many termites. He shows Nik how they rebuilt the house from scratch as a family—Giàu still a toddler.

When he switches to the group chat to show Nik a photo of Giàu, Nik is surprised to find it's the same woman who helped him get drinks at the fundraiser.

"Ella and I had a lot of fun watching you struggle, but Gigi insisted on saving you."

Gigi, Nik notes the nickname. He knows he can't keep it all, but he wants to remember as much as possible.

Nik listens as Vasco tells him about his first attempt at college and why he didn't make it. "I told everyone I got sick and couldn't continue. To this day, even my mothers and friends think that's true." Vasco's screen is black again, but it doesn't matter. The photos are doing exactly what Nik thinks Vasco had in mind: they lead them along as they share themselves with each other.

"Why did you really leave?" he asks, and he keeps his voice low to not ruin the fragile trust that seems to surround them.

"I wasn't ready."

Nik doesn't press him, and Vasco watches the flames for a few moments. "I don't know what I want to do with my life. I thought I did. I was sure I was going to be a teacher, but I really don't like kids. I don't know what I was even thinking when I started studying."

Vasco's hand rubs up Nik's forearm. "I haven't figured it out either," Nik admits.

"Maybe, we can help each other find our paths."

Vasco cringes at his own words, then wakes up the screen and pulls up the next photo. There are many photos of Vasco with his best friends: Eating salad on pizza at the restaurant next to campus, skateboarding underneath a bridge, at the beach.

"I met them at college, but we hit it off from the start." Vasco smiles, as he skims through more photos. He lands on one from what looks like a student party, though Nik has never been to one. "We took up Gippy a few weeks later."

"Gippy?" Nik asks.

"Ate something funny and insisted he had Gippy stomach. Guess he accidentally used *Urban Dictionary* to translate or something." Vasco laughs. "But don't get fooled by him looking all Vietnamese. He's more Mexican than the three of us put together."

Nik wants to meet them, to learn about Vasco through his family and friends.

When his phone battery alert announces 20%, Vasco speeds up his trip down memory lane, summarizes entire blocks as "Trip to Las Vegas," and "The Selfie Challenge." But he slows down to tell Nik about Josephine, his youngest sister who got adopted only a few years ago, long after they thought their mothers were finally done "collecting children," as Vasco puts it.

"We taught her how to be comfortable in a wheelchair, and she taught us to fight through pain. She's so tough."

Nik learns that Jo suffers from something called Chronic Fatigue Syndrome that sounds a lot like his fibromyalgia, and immediately sympathizes with Jo. Abandoned by her mother in front of a sister's house who couldn't take care of a sick child, despite the large amount of cash in an envelope next to baby Jo.

"They left her outside her aunts house with a letter? Very *Harry Potter* style," Nik jokes, and Vasco laughs.

"Let me guess, you're a Gryffindor," Vasco inquires. Nik hesitates, but doesn't get a word in before Vasco adds, "With strong Ravenclaw leanings."

He wants to ask how Vasco knows this, but this isn't the first time he feels like an open book to Vasco, and instead of making him feel exposed, he feels seen.

"I'm a Hufflepuff-Ravenclaw," Vasco announces, and Nik is sure he's found a fellow Potterhead. The 10% alert lights up when Vasco unlocks the phone yet again, and Vasco skips even more photos with a promise of sharing it all with him over time. The last photo Vasco shares with Nik is from Pride parade this year. The day they first met.

Nik studies the photo. Vasco is surrounded by six very different women, his sisters and mothers. His parents are behind them, hugging as many of their children as they can reach. Rainbows are smeared onto Vasco's cheeks, and he smiles confidently between Jo with her crimson curls and a petite Asian girl Nik now knows is Gigi. His other sisters are there, too: Ella, confident and strong to Jo's right, and Dee who wears a Pride flag as a dhuku, and sits cross-legged in front of her siblings.

Nik chuckles inwardly. He dated an Ethopian girl in college and made damn sure to research terminology. At the time, he had learned to impress a girl. Later, he had soaked up knowledge about cultures as a special interest.

"I can't wait to meet them all," he says.

The person, not the shell

When Nik gets up to grab a charger for their phones, Vasco's back chills a little. Nik returns and plugs Vasco's phone into the speaker. When he lowers himself next to Vasco, Vasco pulls the blanket around them. He molds into Nik's side as if their bodies were shaped to fit. The speakers play the *Scorpions* while Nik narrates his camera roll.

His photos start a tiny bit older than Vasco's, the two years between them shining through. He scrolls past filtered-photos he labels "awful" but stops for the occasional anecdote. Nik smiles when he gets to the first unfiltered photos. He opens up one of a much younger Nik with a man and a woman on either side of him. "This was at a writing workshop I attended. These two are small-time authors who earn a living mostly by creating a fandom and selling workshops rather than actual books. But I was so fucking proud that they considered me one of them. You know, this one reached out to me years later." He points at the man with a buzz cut and a Hollywood smile. "He reached out to me a few years later when his fame based on nothing ran out. Wanted to know how I'd landed the book deal, the magazines."

He scoffs, and Vasco sees a lingering hurt about the disillusioned idol.

Nik swipes the photo away and chuckles at one of himself at a convention. "I was so out of my element. I had no fucking clue what I was talking about, but my publisher had a booth there and they sent tickets to all of us. I don't know if you've ever been to a book convention, but it's a huge mess."

Vasco learns that Nik has a lot of past lives. The first life was his time as a small-town journalist, writing stories he hated about events he didn't care about. "I'd convinced myself that I enjoyed what I was doing. But the truth is, I was good at it. That was all. I was fucking good at it. People loved my stories. They said I found details other people never noticed. But I hated it all. Didn't realize until years later, though."

His second life had been as a so-called monkey tester at a company Percy used to work on. "They gave me websites or software to check out with step-by-step tutorials to follow to see if an idiot could use it. My stupidity as a bar for how stupid people are."

Vasco presses into Nik, slides a hand around his neck. "Do you still feel that way?"

Nik shrugs, and Vasco slips a little. "Sometimes."

"I'm sorry for bringing all of this up," he says, because he is realizing that there are people whose camera roll isn't full of happy moments. It was hard to imagine that someone who lived like this could have so much darkness in their lives.

Nik's face lights up when he tells Vasco about quitting that job to go back to university where he bounced around a few subjects, but ended up finishing some communications/environmental science hybrid that even he can't remember the name of properly. "It was called something bullshit that sounds great on a resume. It's been five years and all I've done with the degree is start a blog."

"Do you regret studying?" Vasco asks, and Nik shakes his head. "No. Sometimes. But not really. I learned a lot. I made a few friends, though I lost touch with most of them when they moved all over the country to whatever was next for them. But mostly..." Nik chews his bottom lip, before finishing the sentence. "Mostly, it's about having finished something."

Vasco opens his mouth to answer, but Nik is getting up. "Time to tell you why you brought swim trunks."

"Are you changing the subject on purpose?" Vasco asks. Nik's eyes widen, but he rearranges his expression into his usual neutrality quickly. Vasco has noticed this before. Nik is excellent at hiding his emotions, but if you pay attention, you'll catch glimpses of them, before they vanish behind a mask of not giving a fuck.

"Yes," Nik admits. "It's not that I don't want you to know."

"It's just a lot," Vasco finishes for him, and lets Nik help him out of the hammock. Nik slides a small table and two chair aside, and taps a button on the wall. Light floods out from the floor boards he has just cleared, before the floor sinks down an inch or so and slides underneath the other side to reveal a hot tub. A fucking hot tub on a rooftop patio. His jaw drops, and a feeling of surreality envelops him. There is no way, he's standing here on this patio with a man that makes him smile and glow, about to bath in a hot tub under the stars.

"I thought you might like the stars," Nik says, and Vasco realizes he is watching his reaction.

Vasco looks up at the clear sky, hundreds of starts glittering in the night. "It's beautiful," he manages.

"You don't like it." Nik says it as if it is a fact, not a question.

Vasco walks over to him, cups his face. "It's beautiful, babe. I just can't believe that you live like this."

He feels very self-conscious about his own apartment all of a sudden, the way his kitchen counters are all scratched, the floors crooked, the wallpaper peeling in places. Everything here is polished and—there's no other word for it—perfect.

"Not all that glimmers is gold, or whatever that saying was," Nik says, and there is an edge to his voice. "But I get it. Sometimes, I look around the house and feel like it's not mine, as if I stumbled into another person's life. I don't like it. I don't need any of this. I don't even *want* any of this."

Vasco kisses him, and wraps his arms around him. Nik's arms close behind Vasco's back, and he leans against Nik's chest. "I know," he whispers."I know."

"Let me show you where to change," Nik says gently, and they pull apart.

When Vasco emerges from the bathroom on the top floor, Nik is waiting for him with two fluffy towels over one arm and a bottle in the other. Vasco tries not to stare at his bare chest, the muscular lines, the strong shoulders. Okay, he's definitely staring. And when he forces his gaze to meet Nik's, Nik looks nervous.

The water is hot, and singes his skin when Vasco glides into the water. His skin tingles, and for a moment he feels suffocated all over his body, but then the moment passes, and he relaxes into the warm embrace of the hot tub. Nik stands on the bench and hops around a little, both arms wrangling his dreads into a high bun.

"You want to spray me with water, don't you?" Nik asks when Vasco laughs.

"So badly," Vasco admits, but his hands stay still while Nik continues his slow climb into the pool. Their feet tangle when Nik sits down across from him.

Nik's foot draws circles on his leg, and Vasco leans back to take in the view above. "It's beautiful," he says again.

"The sky is," Nik answers, and Vasco waits for the "but."

Nik sits a little more upright, and Vasco's feet follow Nik's under the water. "I hate it. Not the night sky or the water, but the city. The *McMansions*, the smog, all the buildings. The smells." Nik leans back again, runs a hand over his face. "I want to move somewhere less—" He waves a hand around at the view to their right with its perfectly trimmed hedges and immaculate houses. "Less like this."

"Do you have a place in mind?" Vasco asks, trying not to think about the fact that Nik wants to leave. Some day, he might want to leave to. The idea doesn't scare him as much as it used to.

"You're gonna make fun of me." Nik's beard twitches, as he half-smiles. "Costa Rica."

Vasco sprays water toward Nik, careful not to hit him with any of the spray. Diego said chlorine is a bitch when it comes to dreadlocks.

"Why would I make fun of you for that?"

Nik looks down at the water, steam rising around him, though it quickly gets absorbed into the wind. "I've never been. I don't even really know anything about the country. Fuck, my Spanish sucks badly."

"Te puedo ayudar a aprender español." *I can help you learn.*

Nik looks up with a curious expression, and smiles. It's a hard to describe smile that doesn't break the mask often. When Vasco tries to think of a way to describe it, he sounds as if he's describing Gilderoy Lockhard. It's a very open smile, showing off all of Nik's teeth, including one that's a little crooked. Teasing it out of Nik is worth it the moment he breaks into that warm, glowing, open smile, or that bark of a laugh.

"I'd like that," Nik says, one side of his mouth still smiling. The smile drops, when he asks, "Can I ask you something? I'm not sure it's appropriate. I'm not good with these things."

"These things?" Vasco asks, but doesn't wait for Nik to answer. "You can ask me anything. I'll tell you if I don't want to answer. Take that as a general rule. Ask me anything. Tell me anything. I'll tell you when you get close to a line or cross it."

Nik worries his lip again. "I don't want to cross any lines. I don't want to hurt you."

Vasco scoots forward and lifts Nik's chin with his finger. "Guapo," he says gently. "You will hurt me at some point, and that's okay. We all hurt each other sometimes. Love isn't about finding someone who won't hurt you."

Nik tries to lower his head, and Vasco lets him, places a kiss on his forehead instead. "It's about finding someone who is worth the hurt.

Someone who will talk to you about the hurts, so you can learn from each other, learn to understand each other."

Nik looks up at Vasco, and Vasco sinks into the dark brown gaze. "I want to learn you," Nik says, and Vasco kisses him briefly.

"Me too," he says, before he makes himself sit back to let Nik ask his question.

"What is it?" he nudges.

Nik shifts his lip from side to side, then says, "I don't think this one will hurt you. I just don't want to hurt you in general. Fuck, nevermind. The question: What did you mean when you said your parents were collecting children. Did you mean race?"

Vasco nods. "I'm sorry. That was a thoughtless thing to say."

Nik shakes his head. "No, that's okay. You said your moms—sorry, you used mom and mama, right? What do you call both of them together?"

Vasco laughs. "My parents worried so much about it when they first adopted me. It's cute when I think about it. I usually talk about my parents or mothers, but I've said 'my moms' before, too. My parents don't care."

Nik nods, and Vasco is sure he's filing the tidbit of knowledge away.

"But yes, I meant race. Ella is Indian. Dee is African. Giàu is Asian—yes, I know that Indians are Asians, but we're talking stereotypes here."

Nik holds up his palms. "All good. Your family, your labels."

Vasco laughs, and the steam clears away around him. He watches, as it swirls back, quickly consuming the gleaming blue water's surface.

"I'm Mexican. Sorry, not from Costa Rica."

He gets rewarded by a chuckle from Nik.

"I think we're missing a Russian to complete the cliche. Maybe someone from a small island." He knows he sounds resentful, but he's tired of hiding it. "We're a walking cliche of a diverse family. Fuck, include mama and me—and I think Jo, and you've got the LGBTQ+ spectrum, too."

His voice has risen a little, and he forces himself to take a deep breath.

Nik responds, as if he's never burst. "Your mama wore the trans flag in that photo you showed me."

"Yes," Vasco confirms.

"Can I ask you another question, I'm not sure is appropriate to ask?"

Vasco raises an eyebrow, waits for Nik to grin. "Okay, yes. General rule, right. I'm asking."

Vasco nods, the grin spreading wider.

"When did your mama transition?"

Vasco wants to tell Nik he worries too much, but he saves it for another time, and answer the question. "My mom and her got married when they were just out of college. Excited young couple, ready to take on the world. They started the charity a year or so after, and everyone thought they'd have children. Sorry, this was pre-transition. I should've said."

Nik nods curtly.

"Mama came out to her when they were about to get married. Mama says she couldn't marry her without telling her how she felt. She had waited so long, because she hadn't fully figured out her identity. She didn't want to 'raise the alarm,' as she says, without a reason. But when mom got ready to leave with her bridesmaids, she couldn't do it. She told her she wasn't sure, but that she thought she might be."

Nik's face is neutral, as always, so it's hard to judge if he's getting the mood across or whatever. He hopes, he does.

"And she stuck by her side?" Nik asks, voice a low quiet rumble, like very distant thunder.

He nods. "Mom says she loved the person, not the shell."

Nik's knee bobs a few times, before he looks at their still tangled feet and stops himself. "It's no wonder you turned into such a wonderful man," Nik says after a moment.

Vasco wants to object, a reflex born from years of feeling inadequate, but when Nik says things like this, Vasco feels a little less inadequate each time.

"Thank you?" he says, not sure how else to respond. It's more a question.

"You're so open and accepting," Nik explains, and Vasco tries to believe him. And he does try to be those things. He just doesn't think, he's trying hard enough.

"I'm really glad you texted me out of the blue," Vasco says, his gaze on the sky again.

Nik softly slides his foot up and down Vasco's leg a little, and Vasco feels goosebumps that have nothing to do with temperatures.

And then he realizes something, and lowers his gaze. "How did you text me, now that I think of it."

Nik chuckles. "Percy. She asked her personal assistant who is a magician. I assume the number was taken off the registration for the ticket. Probably against a million privacy laws. I'm sorry."

Vasco waves a hand. "It's fine. I'm glad she did it."

Vasco is almost glad the last few years have broken some of the hard-fought-for privacy laws down in the name of preventing terrorism–or was it protecting the children? Fuck, whatever.

"So, she gave you the number? It's amazing how okay she is with you dating me."

He hasn't really stopped to consider Percy's side in all of this until now.

"She's out on a date with our parkour trainer," Nik says, and Vasco is surprised to find an absolutely unconcealed glee in his face.

He raises an eyebrow, and Nik explains. "I've been fantasizing about them getting it on for years."

Vasco tilts his head, and Nik laughs. "No, no. Not in that way. Without me involved. Yeah, that came out weird. Anyway, I've wanted them to fall in love—better?—for years. Probably since that first day I saw Isavella flirt with her, before I joined them. I mean, they've still been flirting, but always toeing the line, never crossing it."

Nik stands up and climbs out of the pool, turning in slow circles, dripping onto the teak floor. *What the fuck?*

"Nik?" he asks, and Nik's rotation slows.

"The water was getting lukewarm," Nik explains, and Vasco understands. "I'm trying to cool down, so I can enjoy the jacuzzi all over."

Vasco gets up, copies Nik's motion, and is surprised by the chill the air leaves on his wet skin, as he moves.

He grabs Nik's hand, and pulls him in. "Dance with me?"

Nik sways back a little, balancing heel to toe, toe to heel. "Okay," he says.

The implied, "I don't usually dance," or "I don't know how to dance," is heavy in the word. Vasco isn't sure which one it is, but he doesn't care.

"Give me your *Spotify*," he says, almost sure he saw the app earlier when Nik selected music. Nik hands him the phone without hesitation. He selects *Libertango*, and holds out his hand to Nik. He doesn't ask if Nik knows how to Tango.

Nik grabs his hand, and he swirls him toward him. They both laugh, the moment too cliche not to take it lightly: Two people with water droplets glittering like the stars above, swirling through the night in the blue glow of the steaming hot tub.

He guides Nik's hand around himself, holds the other in his. Nik doesn't object, so he leads, even though he is a few inches shorter than Nik, and a lot less strong.

Gently, he presses his knee against Nik's, and Nik steps back. The hand on Nik's hip guides him through steps and sways, and they dance around the rooftop. He bumps into a chair, and Nik stabilizes him, palm strong on Vasco's back. "I've got you."

"I'm not getting any colder, but I like this."

They dance, tango and salsa, kiss in between songs and during a later slow dance. When they glide back into the hot tub, the water isn't what makes his skin tingle. Nik is warm summer rain, soft breezes, and sunshine, and Vasco can't get enough of the man.

"Is it hard for you, with two moms, and the transition?" Nik asks, after a cute internal struggle shining through the cracks.

Vasco shrugs. "It's exhausting sometimes. People always assume. I've never really understood why it's such a big deal."

Nik pulls his lip in between his teeth. "I don't know what the big deal about gender is. It's like race. I don't know why it matters so much." He stiffens slightly, and the water ripples around his shoulders. "I don't mean that it doesn't matter. Culture does. Heritage does, to a degree. I just don't know why people rank them."

Vasco smiles at Nik. "Don't worry. I know what you are trying to say, and I agree. I mean, I've always known that I'm a man. I've never been unsure about that."

"I have," Nik admits. "I considered going by they/them pronouns for a while, but the grammar is so exhausting, and I just don't care enough either way, and I feel male most of the time." He drags a palm over his face. "Damn it, now I sound like a cliché, because I'm bisexual and sometimes feel feminine. Fuck, I hate it when I fulfill prejudices."

"Even gay people get to act gay sometimes," Vasco says. "It's something Jesus said to me once. I was worried that I was being too obvious, too cliche, and he explained that I could be as cliche as I want. 'If anyone deserves to be gay, it's gay people, right?' he said."

"He sounds like a nice guy," Nik says.

"They all are. You'll meet them."

"Not anytime soon," Nik says, and Vasco regrets reminding him of their limitations.

Vasco caresses Nik's feet with his, and chooses his words carefully. "Don't take this the wrong way, but you can be pretty blunt."

"I don't lie," Nik says simply. Vasco is pretty sure Nik has said it before, but if he did, he didn't pause to think about the statement.

He wants to say that he doesn't lie either, but if he's honest with himself, he's been telling white lie after white lie for as much of his life as he can remember.

"I don't want to lie," Vasco says instead, and Nik's dark brown eyes meet his over the steaming water.

"But you do?" Nik asks and there is no judgment.

He nods. "Yes."

Nik slides around the bench until he's next to him. He puts a hand on the pool's edge, behind Vasco's back like a teenage boy at the movies does with the seats, as if their bodies didn't touch skin-to-skin while they slow-danced. Vasco's hand finds his over his shoulder, and he guides Nik's arm around himself.

Nik squeezes his shoulder. "I used to."

"What made you stop?" Vasco asks, as he leans back and closes his eyes. The Santa Ana winds cleared the clouds and the smog of the city, and the sky is as clear and starry as it was when they first met. He scans the constellations until he finds *Ursa major* and still feels accomplished when he does.

"I watched a show where the main character couldn't lie. Well, couldn't isn't—Well, he was just extremely bad at it. Every time he successfully pulled off a lie, he'd get so excited that he'd tell on himself immediately." Nik leans back, his head next to Vasco's, and they look up at the glittering stars. "I guess, it made me realize how much I rely on lies and pretending to be someone I am not."

Vasco decides that he likes the concept. "I want to give it a try," he announces, and he means it.

A ringing makes both of them jump. "Shit, shit," Nik swears, and scrambles for his phone. "Percy, fuck. How late is it?"

His face is eerie in the light of his phone when he unlocks the screen, tinged pink, then white. He watches as Nik steels himself, collects his thoughts. Vasco can almost see him select the right words and arrange them into a sentence.

"Would you like to meet my wife?"

I hate it when you logic

Fuck, fuck, fuck. He hovers, while Vasco hesitates, lips hanging slightly open. "Yes, I think I'd like that."

He isn't sure either of them—any of them—is ready for this, but it is happening, so they change into clothes, and Nik closes up the jacuzzi. They even have time to return the wobbly table Percy likes so much to its proper place.

Nik finally gets around to pouring them the whiskey he carried upstairs earlier, and they talk little while they drink, a slight buzz blurring the edges of Nik's preoccupation with the imminent meeting.

When the front door opens, and Isavella follows Percy inside, he sighs in relief, and Vasco's lip curls the tiniest bit. Vasco has a thousand smiles, each a subtle variation, a slightly different truth. He is intent on cataloging them all, on learning every feature of this man.

"Hey!" Isavella waves at them, not the slightest trace of nerves. Percy greets Marvin who wobbles into the room from what he expects was Percy's bedroom where it is coolest and darkest. She straightens, and Nik notices the slightest tremor before she grabs Isavella's hand and leads her over to the men.

Vasco gets up, and Nik follows suit, a general feeling of awkwardness growing inside him. It's Percy who takes care of the introductions, and Nik is grateful. Vasco and Isavella bump fists and exchange a few lines in Spanish—apparently immediately aware of their shared roots.

Their cheerful greeting breaks the tension, and Nik relaxes a little. "You want drinks?" he asks, raising his own glass.

Percy grabs tequila from the kitchen, pours for herself and Isavella. "How did your date go?" Isavella asks, her usual cool unbroken. Vasco leans around his arm chair to face her. "Did you know there's a hot tub up on that roof?"

"Oh, I love hot tubs!" Isavella cheers, rubbing her palms. "I haven't been in one since a trip to Joshua Tree with my sister a few years back. Can we? I even have a swimsuit in my gym bag. Oh, please, Perce," she begs like a toddler, even though Percy's face makes it absolutely impossible to miss that it is unnecessary. Percy is grinning at her, sparkling pink hearts almost visible, and Nik feels a pang of jealousy that she never looked at him that way, not really. But then he feels Vasco's knee against his, and the world is okay.

When the women have changed, Nik and Vasco follow them back to the patio, cuddle up in the hammock. Percy and Isavella sit with their back to the McMansions and the invisible sea behind them, and Isavella and Vasco hit it off immediately. Percy and Nik sit back, enjoy the lightness of it all, until Vasco forces them into the conversation, gentle nudges that Nik can't ignore.

When Isavella announces she's shriveling up like a raisin, Nik grabs them towels, and they sit around the fire table, the stupid fake flames lighting up their faces. It should be awkward, but even Nik can't get weirded out by the situation.

It's past midnight, when Isavella decides it is time to leave, but makes them promise to meet again. "We can use each other as cover," she says with a mischievous grin. "Vasco's cute," she dimples. "I don't mind pretending to date his ass."

Vasco decides to follow her cue, and Nik leads him into his room for a kiss good-bye—something he's not really comfortable with in front of Percy yet. He'll get there. He's sure of it.

"It's not a bad idea, you know?" Vasco whispers, small kisses on his neck, but always careful not to linger in place.

"You won't be able to hold your breath, when we let ourself go beyond a second first date," he whispers, and feels Vasco's beard twitch against the nape of his neck. And then he realizes what he's said, and he splutters, but Vasco presses his lips on his, and kisses away the urge to apologize. "I'll learn," Vasco says, a new smile tugging on his lip, one Nik can't read yet, but his heartbeat quickens, and the way he kisses Vasco is hungry.

They fall into each other, and Nik feels as if the universe is spinning around them. A moment later, Vasco pushes off Nik's chest with his palm, and takes an unsteady step back. "Not on our first date," he says with a soft smile, but his breaths are shallow, and Nik knows this wasn't easy. "You didn't want to skip any steps, remember? Also, your fancy-ass driver will be here any moment."

Nik groans in frustration, but holds up a palm. "I hate it when you logic."

They both chuckle. "I love it when you grammar."

Nik shakes with laughs, and they share another kiss, giggling as if they are teenagers, and this is their first love. "Good night, Nik," Vasco says, and gently disentangles himself from Nik. "I'll text you when I'm home."

Nik walks Vasco to the door and leans against the frame until he's out of sight. The night air has chilled a little, but the Santa Ana winds are doing their thing well, and he is tempted to turn on the AC. Sometimes, he wishes, he didn't care about this fucking planet.

He washes his face and arms with cold water, lets it evaporate off his arms on the kitchen balcony—yes, another one. There's an unbelievable three balconies and a rooftop patio on this fucking house.

A slight draught makes him look around at Percy, empty glass in hand. "Can I join you?" she asks, and he grunts noncommittally.

She sets the glass down on the railing, and Nik grabs it, before it can fall into the yard below. She slips both hands into the pockets of her robe, and produces Nik's favorite whiskey, her favorite tequila.

They sit down in the camping folding chairs that they never replaced, remnants from their time away from the family fortune. A time that had been supposed to be an adventure but had never felt like one to Nik. Adventure isn't all that adventurous when the safety net of millions is a call to daddy away.

She pours him another drink, and Nik tries to remember how much he's had. He's not drunk yet, he knows that much, but he's definitely getting tipsy.

"Isavella took it well, I assume," he says after they clink glasses. Percy's cheeks flush immediately, and the embarrassed grin on her face answers before she does.

"She told me she's had a crush on me since day one. That she only held back—"

Nik tips his glass toward her. "I *told* you." He even adds a jubilatory "Ha."

"Having her"—he holds up air quotes—"'date' Vasco is a good idea," he repeats Vasco's words to her.

"It's a risk," she says in a monotone. There's always light in LA, but surrounded by trees, it is dark around them, and he can't see her face clearly.

"We don't have to decide today."

He pushes off the railing, squeezes her shoulder, and walks inside.

Teach me

They don't get to see each other again until the next Friday, but they text, and Nik calls Vasco every night. They talk until Nik is tired, and Vasco tells him good night in Spanish, because Nik has finally admitted how much he likes it.

Every day, he teaches Nik new words, and while Nik refuses to form sentences, he picks up vocabulary and phrases. He buys a copy of *The Little Prince* in Spanish, and proofs to Vasco how much he can understand by finishing it within days, a long list of vocabulary on his desk.

During a lecture on ecosystem modeling that is so above his head that he doesn't stand a chance of following, he texts Nik. Nik asks about the class, and his phone buzzes madly enough that he has to silence it fully, when Nik tells him about the sea otters in Morro Bay, kelp forests vanishing around the Channel island, and essentially writes half his report for Vasco over text. He'll have to look up sources later, but he's got half the facts covered already, and they haven't even started research.

He group-texts the guys even though they are feet away, shares his ideas, though he stretches the truth when he says a friend told him about them.

The heart and eggplant emojis they spam into the group make it plain none of them have missed that he's been seeing someone. They don't push him, though, and he madly respects them for their patience. When he came out to them, he had worried a shitton about their dynamic changing, but it only shifted their jokes a little.

On Wednesday, Vasco meets Nik, his wife—he should really stop calling her that—and Isavella at the parkour gym, where he spends an hour getting sweaty and gross, and very self-conscious of how little he's worked out lately. Okay, fine, he's never really been the type to work out.

"I hope you didn't feel pressured to come here," Nik says later when he opens the door to the changing rooms. He worries his bottom lip, teetering on the edge of saying more, and Vasco waits for him. "You don't need to be strong."

But Vasco isn't doing this for Nik. He's doing it for himself. "I've had a lot of fun," he says in lieu of an answer.

They don't shower a the gym in unspoken agreement that this is not how they want to see each other naked the first time. When Nik hugs him good-bye at the train station, he's very self-conscious of how sticky his skin is. But Nik strokes hair out of his face, and kisses the salt off his forehead, as if it doesn't matter. And because of Nik, it doesn't.

He showers at home fifteen minutes later, hot water washing away the sweat. Steam rises in his shower, and he sees Nik's face above the glittering blue of the hot tub, most of him hidden in clouds of vapor. He remembers their kisses, the way Nik seemed to devour him when they kissed that night in his room.

His body responds, and he gives in to desire, lets himself imagine what Nik and him haven't done. He's out of breath when he turns off the faucet, vaguely aware that he's let the water run too long. He's glad Nik won't know how much water he's wasted, because he was horny.

Two parents running a foundation to help charities, many of which dealt with the very real consequences of climate change, and a boyfriend—yes, he's decided to think of Nik that way, though he's not sure when it happened—who doesn't eat meat, wears his hair in one of the most environmentally-friendly ways possible, and knows about little issues most people wouldn't care to listen to. But Vasco is listening, learning, seeing a world he already thought of as beautiful, as precious now, too, because Nik has made him see it that way.

Did you know that the Maori have a king, well currently a queen, to fight against colonial oppression. It's not a hereditary position but the current queen is the daughter of the king before her and her grandmother was the first queen before him, Vasco texts him a few days after Nik let it slip that he's part Maori. "You're a person of color, man," Vasco had cheered. "That's cool! You're the whitest person of color I've met—okay, no, that's not true. There was this petite blonde girl, gringa as you can be, in a Youtube video who was part something."

"Native American," had Nik supplied as if it was a well-known fact, a grin on his face. "I binged the channel for weeks after I found that video of the three grandmas smoking pot for the first time."

Vasco had laughed loud enough to worry about the time and the neighbors. "No way that one grandma wasn't getting stoned all the fucking time."

"She was in it for the free weed, for sure," Nik had agreed.

When his biodiversity teacher tells them about the Maori octopus, he snaps a picture and sends it to Nik who immediately points out that the Maori octopus isn't even endemic to New Zealand.

He sends another fact two days later, and get an article about the Americanification of Mexican culture in Yucatán from a newsletter Nik read that morning in return. They share these tidbits from one-liners to books, each pretending to be annoyed by the other, but they both know they are secretly soaking up every fact; two all-California men of minority heritage who know little about where they came from.

I want to visit, someday, he admits in a text that responds to a documentary Nik recommends.

I'll come with you, Nik promises moments later, and Vasco wants to go over to see him, but he has to finish work for school, figure out how to model a fucking ecosystem, write a few papers. The boys request some of his time, as well, and he meets them to lose at board games, or beats Jesus at Mario Kart on the dented *Wii* they saved up for together last winter.

But finally, after days that felt like years, he gets to see Nik again. Tonight is their second or third date, depending on how you want to count that first one or their workouts at the gym with Isavella and often Percy.

"Where's Marvin?" he asks when he finds Nik alone outside his apartment door. Nik with his half-smile and sharp angles, broad shoulders revealed by a black tanktop, and calves Vasco can almost feel moving up his legs now. Damn it, Cohen, pull it together.

Nik's smile deepens, and he steps over the threshold. "Percy's keeping her at home. Isavella is bringing Sparkles."

Vasco chuckles, and raises an eyebrow. "Why doesn't it surprise me, that the woman has a dog named Sparkles." He holds up a palm. "Let me guess, a chihuahua?"

"Worse, a tiny little thing that looks like it's walked into a wall—or ten. Tiny pug with giant eyes and a sparkling bandana around her chubby little neck."

Vasco takes Nik's hand, and leads him to the couch. "You adore the thing, don't you?"

Nik makes a begrudging sound. "I hate how much I like the little shit dog."

He grabs beers from the fridge, hands one to Nik, and pours chips into a bowl. "Have you made up your mind about the movie?"

"You can choose," Nik answers, so Vasco picks up his phone and asks for a random number between 1 and 5. Four apparently translates to *Contagion*, a 2011 movie that got a huge revival during the first pandemic in 2020. Though, technically, it wasn't the first pandemic, of course, just the first of the generation. The movie's 3.5 star rating seems accurate, and they end up talking through most of the movie.

When the credits begin to roll, Vasco shuts down the TV, and sets the remote aside. He leans against the side of the couch, and slots his legs in between Nik's on the cushions.

"How nervous is Percy about this presentation thing?" he asks after a sip of his second beer.

Nik's eyes say more than his words, and Vasco knows Percy is falling apart. "She's managing." After a moment, he adds, "Isavella is keeping her together, but I really think we better figure out how to get you two a reason to go to that fundraiser. I'm not sure I am any help."

"And I'll have to find a reason to get my tux from my mother's house." He thinks for a moment. "I'll get Ella on it. She already knows about you, so she might as well help us get away with it all."

Nik strokes his thump over Vasco's arm, a slow trail up to his shoulder, over his neck, and along his jaw. "Come to think of it," he says gently after a moment. "What if both of you come to represent your parents' company. You'll bring Isavella as a date, but if Ella's there, no one will think twice about it."

It's true. With Ella working for their mothers' foundation, her presence at one of their biggest contributor's gala would make things a lot easier.

He kisses Nik's fingers, when they touch his lips, and asks quietly. "What the fuck's a pre-holiday gala, anyway?"

Nik shrugs, his fingers tangled in Vasco's hair. "Fuck if I know. It's like with teenagers and parties: they just need a reason to throw a ball."

"So, there will be another one for the holidays?" he asks, half-jokingly, without pulling away from Nik's caresses.

He leans into Nik, foreheads touching, eyes closed. "Probably," Nik answers, barely more than a whisper. He takes a deep breath, and on the breath out, says, "This one's the one that matters, though." He shivers, when Vasco kisses his nose, his eyebrow, his temple. "It's when all the decisions are made," Nik continues, obviously distracted. "Votes and shit happening soon after."

Vasco opens his mouth to ask more, but Nik kisses him, slow and firm, and for what feels like forever. They break apart, and Vasco slides a hand underneath Nik's shirt, traces his muscles up to his chest, where he rests his palm.

"Teach me," he says simply, all traces of the earlier conversation forgotten.

Nik doesn't ask what to teach, leans over to kiss Vasco's cheek. Slowly, he kisses up his cheek to his ear. He grabs Nik's hand, and Nik squeezes it. Something changes in Nik's posture, and Vasco knows the hot open-mouthed breath that follows is what Nik doesn't want to feel. To be honest, he's not the biggest fan of it either.

"If I turn away, don't take it personally, okay?" Nik asks, and Vasco wants to kiss the trembling in his voice away. His lips find Nik's and his answer doesn't need words. He says them anyway.

"If you don't like anything, tell me, or show me," he requests. "I never want you to do anything you don't enjoy."

Nik's next kiss is different, more trusting somehow, and Vasco kisses him back.

"I am nervous," Nik admits when they break apart.

Vasco doesn't need to ask what Nik means, because both of their breaths are shallow and quick, and the way Nik looks at him can only be described as hunger.

"There's no pressure to do anything, Nik."

Nik nods, anchored by his own name from Vasco's mouth. "I know. I—" He kisses Vasco's brow again, the side of his head, nibbles his ear so affectionately that Vasco releases a sigh. "I want to."

"Take as much time as you need," Vasco insists, and he means it. His body might be set on an orgasm, but he wants this to be right, to feel right, for both of them. Whatever exactly *this* is going to be.

He pulls Nik closer, and there is too much fabric between them. He wants to pull Nik's shirt off, but he rubs his hands up Nik's back instead. Nik's smile breaks their kiss. Vasco sways when Nik leans back enough to take off his own shirt, and Vasco can't help but stare at the strong lines, the chest he wants to bite, the thin line of hairs traveling from Nik's belly button downward.

He's distracted long enough, that he doesn't notice Nik's hands fumbling with Vasco's shirt buttons until half of them are open. Nik struggles with the next one, and after an annoyed groan, pulls it over Vasco's head. They both laugh, and it clears the tension a little.

He grabs Nik's hand, gets up from the couch, and pulls Nik up with himself. "I hope, I'm not reading this all wrong," he mutters, as he heads for his bedroom.

Nik catches him around the waist, presses a kiss onto his cheek from behind. "I don't think you are reading any of this wrong," Nik answers. Strong hands turn Vasco's hips, until he's facing Nik, and Nik is kissing him with fire on his tongue. Vasco feels himself being pushed against a wall, the tight embrace and longing kiss pushing more blood away from his brain and into his pants. Or however that works. He's definitely not thinking clearly.

Nik's lips leave his, and he wants to follow, but when Nik trails kisses down his neck, he leans his head back instead. Fuck, this feels good.

Nik nibbles lightly on his chest, his stomach—and he feels self-conscious for a split second until Nik digs his face into the extra pounds, and makes him almost believe he could be the most beautiful man on this planet. Vasco grabs Nik's head, gets tangled between dreads for a moment. He figures it out, and when Nik bites his belly, Vasco pulls him closer.

Nik opens the button to Vasco's jeans, and they exchange a look. Whatever his face is doing—he's not really in control—must have been the right thing, because Nik is pulling down his pants, and he wriggles his feet to free them, throwing them somewhere with one foot.

Nik kisses his stomach again, grabbing his thighs with searching palms. Vasco's dick twitches in his boxers, and Nik giggles against his hip. Somehow, Nik manages to make giggling hot, and Vasco can't help but pull him up for a kiss.

Their bare skin seems to spark between them, and Vasco's fingers explore Nik's back. Both of Nik's hands find their way into the boxers and back around Vasco's cheeks, and Vasco feels both as if he's being claimed and as if he's doing the claiming.

"Guapo," he breathes, and he catches a glimpse of Nik's smiling face, before Nik's face is next to his, teeth closing gently around his ear lobe. Nik's hands move up Vasco's back, as Nik's trail of kisses moves down toward the line of Vasco's boxers.

"Tell me, if I don't know what I'm doing," Nik says, and Vasco doesn't get time to respond, before his boxers hit the floor.

I'm too heavy for this shit

Nik doesn't need to speak any language to understand the words flying from Vasco's mouth, and he lets Vasco's body guide him. When Vasco's knees give a little, he catches him, picks him up by the hips, and guides Vasco's legs around himself. Vasco laughs, and holds on tightly.

"I'm too heavy for this shit," Vasco complains, but Nik doesn't care, and he's carrying Vasco through the bedroom door. He catches glimpses of the room, but as soon as his eyes lock on the bed, his distraction turns to dedication.

Dropping Vasco onto the bed is a little less gentle than he hoped, and he admits, "Maybe a little heavier than I'm used to."

There's a flicker on Vasco's face, and Nik quickly keeps talking. "Sorry, I wasn't talking about—I'm not comp—"

Vasco's gets up and his kiss is urgent. It shuts him up entirely. Vasco's palm against his chest pushes him away gently, and Nik's worry resurfaces briefly, before Vasco's eyes find his—deep green sparked with lust. Vasco sits back down on the edge of the bed, a knee on either side of Nik's legs, face close to—fuck!—Nik's dick, which is rock-hard inside his boxers. Vasco's hands grab his thighs, as he kisses the skin just above Nik's pants. A finger traces the same line on his back, gently searching.

Nik tenses slightly, when Vasco's hand finds its way into his boxers, and Vasco stills immediately. "We don't have to," Vasco begins, but Nik shakes his head. "I want to," he murmurs, his fingers tangling in Vasco's hair. Vasco's gaze lingers for a moment on his, then slowly moves downward, and Nik thinks he should feel self-conscious, but there is no judgment in Vasco's eyes, just longing and something Nik doesn't dare interpret yet, something glowing and warm that seems to be spreading in his own chest, as well.

"You're sure?" Vasco asks against his hip, and his fingers are hesitant. But when Nik grunts, Vasco doesn't slide his fingers back underneath the hem of his pants. Instead, he grabs a fistful of the fabric on either side and pulls. His pants pool around his ankles, and he kicks them off, suddenly strangled by the constraint.

Vasco's palm against his hard dick drags him from his preoccupation with pants, and a gasp escapes him. Vasco's grin is crooked and unreadable, but there is no time to worry or think, because Vasco is pulling down his boxers, and he's naked, and being touched by a man he can't get enough of.

Nik sways when Vasco leans his face into the crook of his leg, caresses the sensitive skin with his lips, and when those very same lips close around his cock, he stumbles a little. Vasco laughs, the same careless giddy laugh, Nik loves so much, and pulls Nik onto of himself.

Nik lands on top of him, a knee between his, a crushing kiss, searching fingers, moans, and gasps that make Nik arch into Vasco. Nik digs his hands into Vasco's hair, pulls himself impossibly closer unable to touch all the places he wants to touch, and when Vasco's hips arch up to meet his, a mumbled "Fuck" escapes him.

The air is thick with hunger and swear words, as they explore each other's bodies. After Nik finishes, Vasco lets him trail kisses down his chest, and Nik finishes his first blow job. He spits, and Vasco pulls him up for a kiss. Vasco's tongue slips into his mouth, and Nik can taste the cum on both of them.

He lets himself collapse to the side, and they lie facing each other on Vasco's sun-faded sheets.

"That was...," he begins, not sure how to find the words, but none of it matters, because Vasco is looking at him with those eyes that don't seem to know how to judge, because Vasco's warm palm is resting on Nik's hip, because they are here. So, Nik lets the sentence trail away.

I have a boyfriend

They lie quietly on top of his blankets, feet dangling off the side of the bed for a few long moments, before Nik turns his head toward Vasco.

Vasco shifts to face him, and the look in Nik's eyes makes that mushy feeling inside his chest grow. No matter how much he used to pretend to be straight, there is absolutely no fucking way that's true. He loves this man. Oh. *That* mushy feeling.

"Te quiero," he hears Nik say, and for a moment, he's convinced he's imagined it, but then Nik keeps talking. "Estoy enamorado."

Vasco is stunned into silence, too overwhelmed by that warm glow that is threatening to make him burst. *I love you. I love you. I love you.*

But before he can say it out loud, Nik is tensing.

"Did I do it wrongly?" he asks, self-consciousness threatening to make his voice stumble over itself. "I'm sorry. Did I say something stupid? I've been overthinking this and I wanted it to be special." He runs a hand over his dreadlocks, and Vasco wants to speak, but his chest still feels so overwhelmingly warm and suffocating. "I thought you'd appreciate it," Nik continues. "I was trying to say I lo—"

And then finally something clicks into place, and his body moves without thinking. He pushes a giant kiss onto Nik's lips to shut him up. It's more a smooch than a kiss, and when they break apart, he sees Nik's confused look, and is glad to find his mouth working again.

"I love you," he says. "Te quiero."

He kisses Nik again, and puts all of the feelings that are expanding in his chest into it. The kiss is nothing like their earlier kisses, soft where those were urgent, giving where they were demanding.

"I love you," he says again when they break apart.

"Did I do it wrongly?" Nik asks again, but there is no more panic in the words.

Vasco shakes his head. "No, I just never thought I'd hear those words in Spanish."

He doesn't know how to explain it. Nik lifts his head onto his elbow and Vasco melts under the undivided attention of those golden brown eyes.

"Do you want to tell me?" Nik asks after a moment. Vasco shrugs, but then considers. "I think so," he says after a moment. "I'm just trying to figure out the right words."

Nik rests his forehead on Vasco's for a moment, before pulling away again. "Okay."

The golden eyes and that mane of dark brown curls vanish from his sight, and he turns his head a little to find Nik rolling onto his back. But before he can even worry about a thing, Nik's hand grabs his own, and he knows Nik is giving him space to think.

"When my parents adopted me, I was six. I'd been in foster care for two years, and could barely remember my parents or my family or anything. I could barely speak any English, and no one there understood me. So, I didn't speak at all."

Nik's hand tightens over his.

"When my parents showed up at the foster house to meet me, neither of them spoke any Spanish either, but they sat down and took the time to listen to me anyway. When they picked me up a few days later, mom greeted me in Spanish. They taught me English, and they got up early to study Spanish." He glances over at Nik who is watching him. "They wanted to make sure I didn't lose touch with my heritage."

He swallows hard through a lump in his throat. Nik places a kiss on his forehead, before returning his gaze to the ceiling. "With each kid they adopted, there were more traditions, more languages, more ways to split their effort. I barely spoke any Spanish for years. I'd listen to Spanish songs or read books in Spanish, but it wasn't until I got to college and met the guys that I got to really speak it."

Nik's voice is soft and low, when he answers. "I bet it's different speaking with native speakers, too."

He nods. "My parents did what they could."

He doesn't say that it wasn't enough. He doesn't have to. Nik's thumb draws circles on his skin, and Vasco turns onto his side.

Nik kisses Vasco's shoulder, and whispers, "I'm no native speaker either, but te quiero, Vasco."

The way Nik says his own name makes his skin tingle.

"Te quiero, guapo," he responds, but his voice barely carries. Nik pulls him closer, and after another long kiss, they lie there, facing each other, content to just exist in each other's space.

"I've never cared this little about messing up my sleep schedule," Nik says after a long while.

Vasco shuts his eyes, sinks deeper into the embrace. "You could stay, you know?"

Nik breathes deeply, taking in Vasco's scent, before answering in a voice muffled by Vasco's neck and shoulder, "I have to be at a board meeting at 8:30."

"I have to be in class at 9."

"Neither of those are a 'no,' you know?" Nik points out, and in the end, he stays. Nik gets him an extra toothbrush, and offers a shirt to sleep in which Nik refuses. Nik returns the unnecessary chivalry by offering to sleep on the couch—though with little conviction.

Nik turns away after he falls asleep, and Vasco cuddles up to his back for a few minutes, before turning away himself. Nik hogs the blanket but Vasco doesn't mind. It's too hot anyway. But he does grab his giant stuffed walrus from underneath the bed.

"Good morning," Nik grumbles when the alarm rings the next morning, and they begrudgingly get up. Vasco makes breakfast while Nik showers, and they eat together. It's not until he takes a shower himself that he realizes how special it is to feel this comfortable with someone, and he is grinning widely when he returns to Nik minutes later.

He makes fun of Nik later, when they take the train together and Nik almost falls over at every start and stop. "Damn white privilege," Nik groans, after he forces Vasco to tell him why he is laughing. He wants to kiss the pained look from Nik's face, but Nik is married, and you never know what homophobic asshole might be watching. Instead, he settles for placing his hand right next to Nik's on the pole and squeezes a little harder than necessary.

Nik looks up at him from somewhere between their feet, and smiles a little sadly. "I know why your parents decided to dedicate their lives to fighting all this fucking injustice. Class, race," he pauses, then adds "gender, orientation…"

"We have come a long way already. We'll get there, Nik." He hesitates for a moment, because he doesn't want to sound like a stalker. He might have read a few of Nik's blog posts and listened to some of his podcast lately. Okay, definitely. And more than a few. No lies, okay. Right. "And your essay on gender neutrality is part of helping people see that none of this shit matters one bit. You are fighting. We are fighting. We'll get there."

He whispers all this very urgently, and Nik's expression softens a little. Then, a grin tugs on one side of Nik's mouth and pulls it up into a beautifully crooked smile. "You read that?"

Vasco feels his cheeks heat, as he nods. "I also listened to some of your podcast. I don't agree with 100% of what you say—and that's totally okay. I still get where you come from, and the rest is mostly preference or point of view." Another short pause of hesitation, but he pushes on. "Well, and some internalized privilege, but—anyway. What I mean is: You are very talented, and I think you'll be able to change a lot of minds."

Nik shrugs, "I can't even figure out how to reach them."

An idea begins to take root, but he wants to think this through, before he says anything, so he decides on. "You will figure it out. I'll help in any way I can."

Nik gets off a few stops later, and waves at Vasco as he turns away.

"Don't forget to take the Blue line EAST, not west, okay?" he yells after him, Nik already looking a little lost on the platform. But Nik gives him a thumbs up, and walks toward the stairs. He knows he would not have had time to drop Nik off and make it to class on time, so he stuffs down the guilt, and digs out his headphones. Nik will have to get home on his own. It's only this one transfer, after all.

One stop later, he gives in and texts Nik to check in. He doesn't relax until Nik sends back, **I'm on the right train. I asked someone. You can stop worrying now. ;)**

He arrives at uni with enough time to spare that it's worth opening his laptop and working on his biodiversity outlines. Instead, he texts the group chat, and the gang shows up a few minutes later. They only look like they abandoned grooming in favor of spending time with him if you know them well.

"Pendejo!" Diego bumps Vasco's fist, then throws his backpack haphazardly toward their customary seats a few rows from the back.

He thinks about a million ways to tell the guys about Nik, but can't figure out the right one. In the end, he blurts out, "I have a boyfriend," like a complete idiot, and time seems to slow down, as he watches them turn, their reactions unfold.

Jesus is first to answer, "That's awesome man."

Gippy slaps a palm onto his shoulder. "I'm glad you're finally ready to tell us what we've known for weeks."

Vasco splutters. "I'm sorry. I should've told you."

But the grins on his friends' faces make it very obvious that they are happy for him, that they understand why it took him so long.

Diego worries his lip for a moment, his brows crunched together. "I'd usually pull some inadequate joke about boob size to get your face into that adorable embarrassed face. But I can't come up with an equivalent that doesn't make me sound gay myself, so I'm gonna shut it. Insert dick joke here."

Vasco laughs. He has heard quite a few of his new-partner jokes each time one of them starts seeing someone.

By the time, the first people start trickling into the lecture hall, he's told them everything that isn't a strict secret. He doesn't lie to them about the rest, and after some poking, they accept that he can't say more. Not yet, at least.

We're losing the Artic

To say the meeting was a disaster is putting it mildly. When it's over, he can tell how much it costs Percy not to run from the room. With determined steps, she leaves the room and heads for her office. He reluctantly shakes a few hands on the way out, utters a few polite content-less phrases, then rushes after her.

He only gets lost twice and is about to head into the correct corridor, when Percy appears around the corner. "Sorry, sorry. I forgot how easily you—Sorry!"

As soon as they've made contact, she turns on her heels and rushes back toward her office. The moment Nik closes the door behind them, she slumps against it, slides down to the floor. She kicks her heels off with her toes, and Nik wonders how no heels get damaged in the process.

He crouches next to her, but doesn't know what to say, so he turns his back to the door and mimics her pose. When Percy still doesn't speak, he sorts through the options in his mind, trying to figure out what the best thing to say might be.

When he's just about to speak, she chuckles, a desperate eerie sound, and he looks at her instead. "I don't think I need to point out that didn't go so well, right?"

He purses his lips. "How bad is it?"

She doesn't meet his gaze, still resolutely facing her own toes. "We're losing the Artic."

He doesn't press her, lets her sit in silence with her head leaned against the door frame, until she is ready to pretend to be okay. When she stirs, he opens his eyes, and lifts his head to see her pull her legs underneath herself. She lifts herself up and forces her feet back into the heels. He accepts her offered hand, and lets her pull him to his feet.

"Let's get out of here. I'll explain in the car."

She doesn't take him past the front desk but instead tells her assistant she's leaving and leads him through the first exit they see. Sunlight makes Nik smile two staircases and a heavy steel door later. They emerge onto a lawn behind the company, and Percy leads him across the grass and onto a tree-lined path that leads them around the building and back to the parking lot.

Percy lets Nik drive—he's a worse passenger—and explains just how bad the situation is. He drops her off at the gym where they both hope Isavella will be able to calm her down, and texts Vasco from the parking lot: **When are you done for today? Meeting went badly.**

It only takes a few seconds for the ellipses to appear, and another few moments until he receives the response. **I'm hanging on campus with the guys. No more classes today.**

Can I pick you up? I'm taking Percy's car home.

He doesn't wait for a response, but instead connects his phone to the car radio, and heads toward Santa Monica. Moments later the car's computer voice butchers Vasco's name so badly, he laughs out loud, and almost misses the message.

Pick me up on 16th street. I'll wait near the pool exit.

Traffic is horrible—though light for LA conditions—and Nik gets to Santa Monica in twenty minutes. He tells the car to text Vasco a few minutes before he arrives, and pulls up to the curb outside the public pool soon after. Vasco's waiting outside waving to a group of guys walking back toward a path between buildings.

"Hola," he says as he ducks into the passenger seat.

Nik's entire being seems to glow at the mere sight of the man, and it only gets brighter when Vasco smiles at him, those beautiful golden-brown eyes sparkling.

"Hola," he responds, and he shows Vasco a quick smile, before he returns his focus to the road, and pulls away from the curb.

He fills Vasco in on the way, tells him about the shit show of a meeting, about how Reginald Fucking Bold essentially hijacked the entire thing—again!—until every middle-aged white male in that fucking room thought Percy's concerns were nothing other than hysteria. She might as well have worn petticoats for all the archaical views those assholes held.

"I don't know how she's supposed to turn this around at the fundraiser. They all seem so set in their views."

Vasco places a hand on Nik's leg, and asks reasonably, "But you said that all the shareholders attend that meeting, not just the higher-ups that attend those boardroom meetings Percy drags you to. I'm sure they'll see reason."

Nik stops himself as soon as he realizes he's chewing his lip again. "I wish I had this much confidence in them. I mean, what kind of people invest in the largest US-headquartered oil corporation? Probably not a bunch of tree-hugging hippies."

When he pulls into the driveway moments later, there's already a car in the driveway.

"Looks like they beat us here. Let's see what Isavella thinks about all this."

Oh, you'll like this

Nik opens the door and Vasco wonders if he's trying to be heard to avoid some kind of walking-into-his-wife scenario.

But any fear of that evaporates when they find the women in the living room, crowding behind a *MacBook* on the dining room table. They look up when Nik and Vasco enter, and Isavella's face lights up with a bright grin.

Isavella jumps up and throws herself around a very uncomfortable looking Nik, before holding out a fist to Vasco. Before Vasco can meet her hand, she shrugs and hugs him, as well. Percy waves over at them, and Vasco is glad he doesn't have to figure out how to greet his boyfriend's kinda-ex wife.

"Nik filled you in?" Percy asks, and he nods. Isavella swirls off into the kitchen and returns with two more mugs and a pitcher of water, clearly at home here much more quickly than he is.

Percy types rapidly on her computer, a look of either desperation or dedication on her face—Vasco isn't quite sure. Nik's hand finds his knee below the table, and Vasco places his hand on top of his, careful not to interlace the fingers out of habit.

"Anything new?" Nik asks Isavella in a kind of stage whisper that is clearly supposed not to disturb Percy.

Percy holds up a finger, purses her lips in concentration, and types a few more lines. "I think, I've got it."

She stares at her screen, her lips moving silently down the screen. "Yeah, I've got it."

"Oh, you'll like this," Isavella cheers next to her.

"That sounds like good news," Vasco interprets.

Percy shrugs, "I'm not so sure. Well, it might be. I don't know. Look," she turns her screen, so they can all see it. A cryptic spreadsheet with what looks like color-coded names lights up the screen.

"What am I looking at?" Nik asks, before Vasco has a chance to make sense of anything. "Are those the board members?" Nik squints at the screen. "Yeah, I've definitely heard that name before. But..." He trails off, his face scrunched up.

Percy gestures at the list. "You know how we've been trying to stop the Arctic project from happening?" Nik, Vasco, and even Isavella who clearly knows where all of this is headed nod. "I think we've been going about all of this wrongly. Who cares about saving the Arctic—" Nik looks ready to argue, but she presses on. "Who cares about saving the Arctic if it just means they'll find another project instead. Plus, there's all the other countries fighting over the same territory. Norway and Russia have been at odds up there for decades. Svalbard might be a no-military zone on paper, but—anyway. What I'm trying to say—" She draws in a deep breath. "I think we can do better."

Vasco turns to look at Nik who looks just as flabbergasted as he feels, when Nik asks, "How did we get from certain defeat on the Arctic project to bigger things?"

Twin grins spread on Percy and Isavella's faces, and Vasco is sure Isavella is enjoying the suspense.

"Because," Percy explains after holding the beat for a moment, "I didn't even consider letting go of my inheritance before."

No pressure, right?

Nik feels like he can't breathe even before Percy tightens the ridiculous bow-tie around his neck.

"I hate these things," he says unnecessarily, and he doesn't blame Percy for ignoring him. Wearing dress shoes, ties, and suits to a few fundraisers each year was bad enough but with all the recent meetings, it feels like he's living in the fucking suit.

The door bell rings a few moments later and both Isavella and Vasco join them inside. Nik barely registers how stunning Isavella looks in her shoulder-less bordeaux gown, before his gaze is drawn to Vasco. He's wearing the same suit and tie he did the night they met, and the effect is no less stunning.

He looks Vasco up and down, and then up again for good measure, and when he's taken in his fill—okay, when he thinks it would be creepy to stare any longer—he meets Vasco's gaze. A self-conscious smile tugs on Vasco's lips, but when Nik tells him that he looks amazing, the smile gets amplified, and Nik has to fight the urge to pull Vasco into his bedroom for a very long kiss, and maybe to tear off that dashing suit.

"Ready?" Isavella asks, and Nik remembers that there are other people here. He pulls his eyes from Vasco, and looks at the women.

"Ready," Nik and Percy echo.

The company has sent a car for them and they arrive at the fundraiser half an hour later. When they get out, Nik almost slides his hand around Vasco, but Percy squeezes herself between them, so Nik's arm finds her waist instead.

"Thanks," Nik whispers, before Vasco nudges his elbow and points toward a car further down the line. Ella, or so Nik assumes, in a bottle-green dress and black heels, steps out of the car and onto the sidewalk. When she spots Vasco, she waves and rushes over with a warm smile on her face. Nik takes the excuse to let go of Percy and they welcome Ella into their circle.

"¡Hermana!" Vasco exclaims, when she hugs him.

"Everyone, this is Ella," Vasco introduces and shakes hands with each of them in turn. "Ella, these are Persephone—"

"Percy is fine," Percy interjects.

"Well, okay. Percy, then, and Isavella. And this is Nik."

Ella's eyes soften further when they land on Nik, and she leans closer to him. "I'm very glad my brother has found someone who can keep up with him."

"Gigi will be here any moment," Ella explains, and Vasco's look of confusion mirrors Nik's feelings.

"You picked Gi as your plus one?"

Ella places a hand on Vasco's arm. "Don't worry! She's known about you two for weeks." She shoves Vasco a little. "You should really give her a bit more credit. Mama knows something up, too, but she isn't asking questions yet."

Nik almost swears out loud, but manages to keep his thoughts to himself. He exchanges a glance with Vasco, who is clearly trying to tell him to stay calm, but calm isn't the feeling currently threatening to explode from his chest.

"Don't panic, guapo," Vasco whispers into his ear. "Everything will be fine. We won't have to pretend much longer, and my family is nothing to worry about."

But Nik does worry. He doesn't exactly worry about Vasco's family, but he does wonder if they've been too obvious. He wonders who else might be suspecting something, though he can't come up with a single reason why anyone would know—or care.

He still vows to play his role as Percy's supportive husband well tonight—the damn male the misogynistic pricks from the board need to take Percy even remotely seriously.

Ella points out the second Cohen car a few moments later, and Gigi joins them. Finally at full count, they head inside where black-tied suit-bearers lead women in fancy hairdos and extravagant gowns toward tables. Isavella hooks her arm around Vasco's elbow a few steps into the room, and he slips his hand back around Percy's waist, albeit reluctantly.

They are barely seated, when one of the late-middle-aged white man takes the stage. He opens the event—an honor that should be Percy's as the CEO and the person with almost half of the company's shares. Dinner is served, and Nik digs into a pretty decent vegan burger.

"So," Gigi says, leaning closer to him and lowering her voice conspiratorially. "Ella finally confessed that Vasco has a boyfriend. You must be the reason he's been so happy lately."

Nik shrugs. "I hope I am." He shrugs again. "I don't know. I think I'm making his life pretty damn complicated."

Ella leans past Gigi. "Seems to be worth it." She winks. "I've never seen my brother smile this much."

Nik feels his cheeks warm, but is rescued by Percy, who seems unaware that she's interrupting when she speaks to him. "My speech is right after dinner. Are you sure about this?"

She seems to ask herself the question as much as him, so instead of voicing any of the million doubts in his mind, he nods. "Let's save the world."

Percy laughs. "No pressure, right?"

"No pressure," he answers, and takes another bite of his dinner.

When Percy takes the stage, she take Nik's hand, and he wonders how such a simple gesture can change so much. He's held Percy's hand thousands of times, but his world seems to be split into before and after, and nothing that was right before feels right now.

Now, he wants to shrug off her too-soft hand. Now, he wants to run from the stage, from this room, from all of this. But then he finds Vasco at their table, an encouraging smile on his face, and he knows he can do this.

Plus, he doesn't even have to speak. He stands and smiles while Percy delivers a TED-level talk about the Artic project, focusing very heavily on the environmental impact such an undertaking would have on the planet. She doesn't sugar-coat or stop at anything, and Nik doesn't have to fake his smile when he sees the faces of the board members lose what little color they held.

"I urge you to consider the fates of humanity, of yourselves and those who come after you, when you cast your vote in January. To quote my dear husband—" She raises their joined hands between them. "We are animals. We are no better than the polar bears or the birds. We are no more important than the frogs or the cows. We are animals, and we should learn to act like it."

Nik glows with pride when he recognizes the last lines from one of his essays. The room is silent for a moment, and Nik holds his breath. The board members' stony faces have regained their color and now resemble carrots (or tomatoes?) more than human faces. None of them move, but when Isavella, Vasco, Gigi, and Ella begin to clap, most of the room joins in.

Nik's first thought is "Fucking sheep," but when he looks around the room, he notices that quite a few people are whispering, exchanging glances. And while the table with most of the board members looks thunderstruck, he notices a lot of people—especially those in their *J.Crew* best—nodding thoughtfully.

Giving a shit is expensive

"Dance with me, bella." Vasco holds out a hand to his official date, and after a moment where Isavella continues to watch the dancing couples on the floor, she gets up and follows Vasco, one hand in his, the other tapping the air in tune with the music, rhythm entering her step.

Vasco swirls her once, then pulls her close, but it's nothing like when he danced with Nik. A respectful inch of distance remains between them, as they dance their way past the swaying couples.

Nik holds out a hand to Percy. "Can you lead?"

Percy laughs, but grabs his hand. Ella pulls Gigi from her chair, and they walk toward where Vasco and Isavella are circling. Nik holds Percy's waist as if he's leading, but follows her gentle pushes. He steps onto her toes a few times, mumbles apology after apology, but she shushes him. "Ten years, I try to get you to dance with me." She leans closer, her voice a mere whisper in his ear. "And all it takes is for you to meet a cute guy."

He coughs, splutters, but he knows no one else heard. Still, his gaze drifts over to Vasco, the sway of the man's hips enough to take him back to a rooftop under the stars.

After a few songs, Percy's heels force them to their now-vacated table. They slump into their chairs, and Nik can tell Percy is fighting the urge to kick off her heels. Before he can even consider poking fun at the misogyny of high heels, he notices a man hovering at the edge of the dance floor.

The man fits every cliche of a hipster: from his yellow tie patterned with rubber ducks—Hold on. Yes, yellow rubber ducks on a yellow tie. Why not.—to the exact shade of his brown leather boots and the solid beard. The man's gaze jumps to their table again, then quickly away when he notices Nik looking at him.

A very visible mental struggle later, the man raises a hand and waves hesitantly. Nik suppresses a laugh and waves back. The man sways back and forth two more times, before he seems to mentally steel himself, and his feet carry him to their table.

"Hi," he stammers.

Nik waves a hand at the empty chairs around the table. The man lays a hand on the back of one, but doesn't sit down.

"I am sorry to disturb you. I just wanted to say—" he pulls out the chair and sits after all, before leaning closer to them, and dropping his voice. "I'm sorry. I'm not good at these things." He shakes himself. " I'd like to sell my shares."

It takes a few seconds for either of them to stir, but then Percy seems to find her wits, and responds. "That's wonderful news."

She doesn't ask him how many shares he holds. Every tiny bit counts, and they all know it.

"Why?" Nik bursts out, and Percy shoots him a look that clearly warns him not to scare off their one success story.

"I'm sorry. It's none of my business—" Nik begins, but the hipster holds up a hand.

"It's okay. It's a fair question. I mean, to be honest, the question I ask myself more is why I ever invested in the first place. Though, to be even more frank, I know the answer to that one: money." He sighs, runs a hand through his beard. "When I first started investing, my dad taught me. He said not to invest what we believe in but what works. His logic was that there is a lot more money to be earned by investing in shitty companies, and that you could then invest that money to do good."

Nik scoffs. He's opened his mouth for another apology, but Percy cuts in first. "Did he?"

She claps a hand to her mouth, and the speed of her apology rivals Nik's apology problem. "Sorry, that's not my place. I'm sorry. Ignore the question. None of my business."

The man laughs, a genuine full-chested laugh that makes his beard twitch. "Don't worry. I've called myself a hypocrite for this more often than I care to admit. I know it's bullshit. But pretending not to notice is a lot easier when it brings you a quarterly pay-off."

"I hear you, man," Nik chimes in. "Giving a shit is expensive."

"—and hard work," the man agrees.

"Amen to that." Nik raises his whiskey, drains the glass.

"Anyway, I'd like to sell my shares to do some actual good. And thanks to your speech earlier, I am probably not alone."

Percy blushes, and Nik places his hand on hers and squeezes for some courage. He hopes the hipster investor is right.

"We need a two-third majority in January." Percy squeezes Nik's hand back, confidence back in her voice. "Every share will matter. We're expecting this to be an uphill battle—one we aren't yet sure we can win." She bites her lip, hesitating, then continues. "We'll need a lot of people like you to do the right thing—despite the quarterly pay-out."

"And who knows what your speech will do to the stock market," Nik adds before he can stop himself.

Percy waves a hand at him. "Yeah, and that."

The hipster investor looks defeated for a moment, but seems to pull himself together. "The best moments in history were uphill battles."

Nik decides he likes the man. Rubber-duck tie and all.

"Well, to make sure you sell your shares before an eventual collapse of our stock, lets sit down, so I can talk you through it, shall we?"

She shows him to their table, and Nik excused himself from the conversation, before he gets dragged into anything to do with shares, trading, or Wall Street—yes, that's the extend of his knowledge on this stuff. Instead, he walks around the dance floor, his gaze always returning to where Isavella makes Vasco look unbearably hot.

Vasco's ass in that suit. And that laugh, as he twirls Isavella around. Unbearable.

With feeling plus stuff

"You're vibrating."

Isavella laughs, and pulls back a little, giving him room to fish his phone out of his suit's chest pocket.

Meet me in the bathroom upstairs? Please. It's urgent. With feeling + stuff, Nik.

Vasco steps on Isavella's foot. It's the first time they've broken step since they started dancing songs and songs ago.

"I, sorry. I—" he starts, as Isavella grabs his hip to steady him.

"That's your Nik face." Isavella hasn't known him for long, but either his face is speaking volumes, or she's picked up his expressions quick.

"Yes, sorry. Would you be fine without me for a while?"

She lifts his hand for a final twirl he barely participates in, before leading him back to their table, their joined hands high in the air, as they slalom around the dancing couples.

When he realizes who is at the table, he tucks on her hand. "You go ahead. I'll see you in a bit."

I'm on my way.

When he pushes the door to the bathrooms open, Nik is washing his hands in the otherwise vacated room. The empty room takes him by surprise for a second before he remembers only few people have access to this part of the building.

Nik grins at him. "¡Hola!"

Vasco swallows hard. "¡Hola!"

He stands rooted to the spot, two steps from the door, as Nik walks toward him. He's fucking unbearable in that suit, and Vasco has to work hard not to pull the damn thing off Nik. He reaches for Nik, and Nik embraces him, but leans past him to lock the bathroom door behind them.

Vasco's dick twitches. "Urgent, ey?" He teases, but he doesn't get any further, as Nik's hip presses into his, driving all thoughts from his brain, all breath from his lungs.

"I just have to." Nik's voice is breathless, need tracing through every sound. "Watching you dance. It's… Fuck! It's a lot, man."

"Must be all the feeling plus stuff," Vasco teases, equally breathless. Nik pulls back a bit, but Vasco grabs him by the hip, and kisses him deeply, both of them hard. Nik pushes him against a—thankfully not bathroom-dirty—wall, and Vasco loses track of everything, when Nik drops to a crouch, and unbuckles Vasco's belt.

He lets Nik drown his emotions in a blowjob that makes Vasco grab the sink. After Nik spits into said sink, Vasco pulls him closer for a kiss—and to return the favor. When he gets up again, his knees are wet, because his thighs don't support a crouch for long enough. Well, shit.

Friend

Vasco can't stop laughing long enough to find his phone, because Nik is tangled in his pants. It's not early, but the call still woke them up.

He's got his own phone lodged between an ear and a shoulder, and is wobbling dangerously. Nik catches himself with his butt on the wall and finally manages to put his pants on enough to stand.

"I'm with a friend right now," he explains to a grumble of a voice on the other end. Vasco can't make out any of the words.

"Persephone is doing great. Thanks for asking." Nik has his fake smile turned up to 11, and Vasco wonders who the caller is.

"I don't wanna keep my friend waiting, sir—" Nik makes a quacking motion with his hand. "Yes, quite the news. Yes, thank you. Yes." Nik's face is growing more and more concentrated, clearly moments from losing track of the conversation—or his patience.

He squeezes Nik's shoulder. There's a weird feeling in his stomach that he can't quite parse.

"Sir, I really need to leave. My friend, you know?"

Friend.

Nik finally manages to hang up the phone. He smiles apologetically at Vasco. Vasco can't make himself react.

"Nik, don't take this the wrong way, please."

Nik immediately looks worried. Not what he had in mind. "No." He places a hand on Nik's cheek. "No. It's nothing like that. You just—It's just—" He takes a deep breath. "Hearing you call me a friend kinda hurt, especially because you had to pretend to be happily married—again."

Nik sighs. "I'm sorry." He meets Vasco's eyes. "Lo siento."

Vasco pulls Nick back to the edge of the bed, and they sit next to each other. "I know you had to pretend. I know this hurts you like hell. I know you are probably so much more pissed off by all of this than me."

Nik places a hand on his lips, very gently. "Babe," he whispers. "You get to feel shit about this, too."

Nik slides his hand onto Vasco's shoulder. "I promised, I wouldn't keep apologizing or telling you to get out while you can."

"Too late for that," Vasco says with a smile and a nudge. "Also, that sounded like a but."

"But—" Nik can't seem to stop the grin from spreading. "Yes, yes. But I need you to promise me something in return."

Vasco pulls himself against the wall, his legs across the bed. Nik follows, one leg tucked in. "Promise me, you'll tell me when things are hard. Don't try and protect my feelings."

"Speaking of feelings," Vasco interjects, definitely not changing the subject.

"I know you're changing the subject," Nik says, wiggling a finger at him.

Vasco laughs, decides to push on. "With feeling plus stuff?"

Nik blushes, and Vasco almost regrets bringing up the text. "Are you blushing because we had sex in a bathroom—" Nik's face takes on more color. "—or are you blushing because of your word choice?"

Vasco's gaze follows Nik's Adam's apple all the way down. And back up.

"Both?" Nik asks.

"Most people would have put an ampersand or just spelled out the extremely long word 'and.' Why go for a plus?"

"Don't you have younger sisters?" Nik asks, his face slowly returning to a normal color.

Vasco groans extensively, mock outraged. "Is this another one of those internet phenomenons people keep telling me about?"

"You sound like my batty old neighbor."

Vasco sucks his lips between his teeth. "Und früher war viel mehr Lametta," he says in his best old-grandpa German.

"Yeah, exactly that. What?" Nik looks confused.

"Another German thing."

"Your code-switching sucks, babe," Nik teases. "I don't speak German." After a moment, he adds, "Yet."

Vasco wants to kiss him. Right. Now. But he also wants to have this talk, so he settles for a peck on the cheek, and tells Nik exactly that. "Lo siento, guapo. You're right. I need to tell you when I'm hurt."

He turns to face Nik, leaning his side against the wall, pulling in a leg. "I got hurt. It's not your fault, but it was by your actions. Fuck, I sound like Dumbledore or something." He groans again. The sound vibrates through his chest. "No, not Dumbledore. Fuck it, Dumbledore." Now is not the time to cure his Harry Potter referencitis or talk about that awful transphobic author.

Nik's face flashes through emotions, settles on confusion. "I know we've gotta have this talk, but what the fuck with the Dumbledore thing."

"Don't want to support or spread transphobia." It's that simple.

"I try to separate the story and everything it meant for me growing up from that awful woman. It's got a lot of flaws, but there's also a lot of magic."

Nik takes Vasco's hand without interlacing their fingers, an abrupt return to topic. "I don't care if you sound like Gandalf—yes, yes, I know. Everyone is white and women don't really matter as people. Gotta pick a reference here. I want to hear it." He squeezes Vasco's hands. "Tell me."

Vasco considers returning to their topic, but this text message has been nagging him, so he decides to finish that conversation first. One thing after the other. They have all day.

"You know that 'with feeling + stuff' thing?" Vasco asks, tracing circles around Nik's abs.

Nik grunts. "Yeah."

"I thought you were going Hamilton on me."

Nik jerks upright, knocking Vasco's hand off his belly. "Hamilton."

"You know, it's this musical by Lin-Manuel—"

Nik waves him off. "No, I know. It's just—I love that musical. Going 'Hamilton' on you would be exactly my kind of thing. In this case, no, though." He lies his head back down next to Vasco. "Also, what's the reference."

Vasco sings, "My dearest, Angelica."

Nik facepalms, looking a lot like the emoji. Vasco has noticed a lot of Nik's expressions would make excellent emoticons. Emoji. Whatever. Those smiley things when they don't just smile.

"Don't know if I'm anchored by you Germaning earlier—"

Vasco bursts out laughing. "Germaning?"

"Yeah, it's a word. Or now it is. Neologisms are a thing. Anyway. I wonder how they translated that one. You think every language will have a comma they can move?"

"Meine Liebste, Angelica," Vasco sings, though it's not perfect. "Could work," he judges.

"Does the meaning change?" Nik asks. "If you move the comma, I mean."

"Meine liebste Angelica. Meine Liebste." A pause. "Angelica." Vasco tries it a few more times, seems to think. "Yeah, I think it does actually work. Though my German is a bit rusty."

"Speaking of very bad translations, you wanted to Gandalf about your feelings."

Vasco raises an eyebrow. "I'm not following that segue."

Nik's lip twitches into a half-smile. "I wish I'd ended my letter with the most romantic sentence in all of Shakespeare instead of that lame plus sign thing."

"Tall order. Now I wanna hear that sentence," Vasco says.

"He that thou knowest thine." He lets the words sink in, then explains, "It's from *Hamlet,* and I read it as something like 'he who you know is yours.' To me, it's one of the most romantic sentences ever. It's such a romantic way of ending a letter. Badly translated in the modern-English version, though."

"As?" Vasco barely dares to ask. Bad translations are always so, well, bad.

"Good-bye."

They burst into laughter, but the unfinished conversation pulls them back quickly. "So," Nik returns them to the topic, as they return to their places against the wall. "You wanted to Gandalf about your feelings."

"I love you, Nik." Not very Gandalf, but it needed to be said. "But this isn't a movie. Life often feels like a shitty director was trying to keep a TV show going for too long. I don't want to be your friend. I want to be your boyfriend. Maybe, some day, your husband."

Nik shifts, a gentle smile on his face. Vasco is surprised he doesn't interrupt.

"I want to introduce you to everyone. Not as my friend, but as mine." He remembers when he walked back down to their table after, well, just after. When his knees where stained wet, and Isavella had that knowing look on her face. "Seeing you with Percy on stage, getting introduced as her husband—it fucking hurts, man." His voice breaks, and Nik looks like his heart is breaking, too. "You're mine."

The struggles of the rich

The restaurant door opens with an infuriating ding from the bell above it. In the crowded place, that bell keeps going off. Vasco, despite what Nik calls his never-ending patience, is annoyed by the thing already. Nik would hate it. But Nik isn't here yet, and neither are Percy and Isavella, so Vasco is sitting alone on a bench near that stupid bell.

"May I see you to your table, sir?" a voice with practiced politeness asks him. Or rather, the person the voice belongs to does.

He tells her he's waiting for his party to arrive, but she insists, "Mrs. Simmons called ahead. I'm to tell you that she and her dear husband will be here soon. She asked me to make sure you're well taken care of."

At that very moment, the bell dings yet again, and Isavella enters. He waves a hand, and she joins them. The attentive waitress takes a polite step back, and averts her gaze until they've exchanged greetings, and in the case of Vasco also a bunch of compliments, because that pantsuit she's wearing can only be described as smart.

They follow the woman to a table set for four. They sit, and the waitress fills their glasses with water from a fancy carafe that looks like it costs more than all of his parents' dinnerware.

"Am I the only one tempted to steal this thing?" he whispers to Isavella when the waitress has finally disappeared.

She chuckles, "I had my eye on those fancy tiny spoon things." She points to delicate golden spoons above each plate setting.

"I've never stolen anything in my entire life, but—"

Isavella's face displays mock outrage. "What kind of Mexican are you? Aren't we supposed to all be thieves?"

The waitress returns halfway through yet another long laugh, and Vasco is glad their table is in a separate area of this way-too-fancy restaurant. They school their faces into semiprofessional expressions.

"The rest of your party has just pulled up outside. They will join you in a moment."

They nod their thanks, because both of them are trying too hard not to laugh. They burst the moment the door closes behind the woman.

"I think we might not be the target audience of this place," Isavella continues when they have calmed down enough.

Vasco answers, "Probably not," just when the door opens again. Another waiter, no less practiced professionalism, steps through and holds the door for Percy and Nik. Both of them look rushed and slightly disheveled.

The waiter pulls out Percy's chair for her, and Vasco is again reminded that this isn't his scene.

"If I didn't know any better, I'd say you two are late because you had sex," Isavella jokes the moment they are alone.

Percy, who is halfway through a sip of water, coughs.

"And if I didn't know any better, I'd agree merely from that reaction," Nik adds. "But, I was there." He loosens his tie just enough to breathe while maintaining decorum. "Why we are late is a lot more exciting, though."

Before Nik gets to say more, the door opens and five—yes, five!—of the staff enter. Apparently, Percy is some kind of VIP here, and they all get that treatment today. More staff than guests, one of them the fucking floor manager, from what Vasco can surmise.

He exchanges a glance with Isavella, who is clearly having similar thoughts and fighting silent amusement. No, not the target audience at all.

Percy exchanges words with the lady Vasco though of as the floor manager earlier, and all five staff disappear again.

"I've ordered ahead," she explains, "so we'd get some uninterrupted time to talk, but I have a feeling that won't work as well as I'd hoped."

Nik sighs. "Oh, the struggles of the rich."

Percy shoves him lightly with her elbow. "Whose idea was this double-date thing again?"

Nik holds up placating palms. "Not mine. You can blame these two." He indicates Vasco and Isavella. "They were the ones—"

Isavella interrupts him. "Don't hate on this evening before it's started, people."

Before Nik can even start telling them about, well, whatever he's so excited about, the first course arrives. Drinks are added to glasses, and Vasco finds himself in front of a dark murky beer he didn't order.

When he looks up, Nik is smiling at him. "Did I get it right?"

Vasco takes a sip and can't stop himself from smacking his lips. "That's one damned good ale," he comments, and Nik looks accomplished.

"Can you finally talk now," Isavella urges, while stabbing a small tomato on her fork that keeps trying to evade her.

Nik sits upright, and wipes his palms on his pants, before he finally talks. "I met that dude who called this morning." He looks at Vasco, so he nods, and gestures for him to continue. "I couldn't place the man when he called this morning, only knew he was one of the higher-ups at Bold Industries."

"Heinz Gustav Fritz Robert," Percy supplies.

Vasco laughs. "What a ridiculous name. One first name wasn't enough?"

"For a ridiculous person," Nik adds, then continues his tale. "Well, that four-first-names dude wanted to meet. Supposedly, he's grown a conscience and would like to sell his shares and 'help out.'" Nik mimes air quotes. "Whatever that might mean."

Isavella jumps up and down in her chair, her salad forgotten. "But that's good, right?"

Percy and Nik both nod. "Yes," Nik says, "It's very good."

Percy places a hand on his, and Vasco wonders why the pang of jealousy he'd expect is missing. He wouldn't have been okay with Michael getting touched like that.

Vasco takes a few bites of the salad, but doesn't finish it. He doesn't know how many courses there will be, but thinks the salad might be the least exciting of them. Leaving room and all that.

"We're still down quite a few shares for an absolute majority," Percy explains. "And this a-hole—" Isavella chuckles, and Percy looks at her in surprise.

Isavella chews her food down as fast as she can, and mumbles, "Sorry, chica, but you're so fucking cute when you swear like a third-grader."

Percy grimaces. "Be that as it may," she continues, "We're still short quite a few shares if we want that absolute majority. And this—" She pauses to glare at Isavella, though the gesture is ruined by the grin she's fighting. "*Asshole*, holds five percent."

Vasco's gut reaction is to point out that five percent aren't much, but he swallows that response. "Five percent. It's something," he says instead, reminding himself just how much those five percent are worth. Five percent of a shitton is still a shitton.

"We need every single percent of a percent," Percy points out, and they all know how true it is.

"So, he's giving up all of his shares, just like that?" Isavella asks, but they don't get a chance to discuss this, because the door opens yet again, and their salads are exchanged for a soup.

"Just how many courses are there?" Isavella asks. The waiter who was serving her responds, "Mrs. Simmons ordered the four-course meal, ma'am. Would you prefer another arrangement?"

Arrangement. Vasco wonders briefly if using the most complicated way of saying something is part of the job description. Or do they get trained on how to word things this way?

Isavella splutters incoherently until Percy addresses the waiter. "That's quite alright. We are very happy with the original order. Please, don't trouble yourselves on our behalf."

"And what exactly is this," Isavella asks when the waiter is out of earshot. She's stirring the whiteish soup hesitantly.

"Corn chowder. It's just a creamy corn soup." She tilts her head at Nik. "Vegan version of a clam chowder essentially. I hope you'll like it."

And they do. The chowder, or whatever that thing was called, is delicious, and so are the cauliflower steaks that are served next. Vasco starts to feel full after the soup, but the food is too good to waste. And, he has a feeling doggy bags aren't exactly part of how things are done here.

"The more food I get into myself, the sleepier I get," he admits when the cauliflower steaks are taken away, and they get a break from eating.

Isavella pats her stomach, and Percy laughs, "Good thing they aren't serving desert until we request it. So, bar the millions of check-ins to ensure we are topped up on everything, because we'd obviously die if we're without wine for more than a minute, we'll have a bit of time to chat.

Nik looks around in an exaggerated way, then kisses Vasco's cheeks. "Sorry," he grins, "Couldn't stop myself."

"Beginner," Isavella teases.

Percy points a finger at her. "Ah, Vella, you're forgetting your unfair advantage."

They all look at Percy. "Which is?"

"Boobs," Nik answers, before she can say any more. "They can be all touchy, and no one will think twice. Because—"

"—they are women," Vasco realizes. That was indeed an unfair advantage.

"It's like the staircases in *Harry Potter*," Nik says, and immediately loses the attention of both women. He leans closer to Vasco. "You know, how the founders thought boys couldn't be trusted."

Vasco nods. "And Hermione can get into the boy's dormitory."

"But they can't get into the girl's one, exactly," Nik finishes.

It takes all of his effort not to react to Nik being this close, so he leans back in his chair. With disappointment on his face, Nik follows suit.

"Can we get the fuck out of here," he asks, and pulls Isavella and Percy back into the conversation.

"We can't leave before I've tasted whatever they serve as desert here," Isavella protests immediately. No, no they can't.

But Percy being Percy presses a button on the wall beside them and summons the floor-manager person. Ten minutes later, their deserts are packed up in what can only be described as doggy bags, no matter how fancy the packaging, and they are out of the door and on their way to casa Simmons.

As soon as the car door closes, his hand is on Nik's knee, and he can see Isavella and Percy's fingers intertwine between them on the back seat.

"This is so fucking strange," he says with a wave around the car.

"You're good at stating the obvious," Isavella pokes. "Can't wait to not pretend to date your admittedly cute ass."

"Oh," Nik's voice is mischievous. "You'll have your hands full actually dating that woman."

Percy's mock outrage gets shot down with a kiss from Isavella, and Vasco hates himself for checking the surrounding streets for people who might have seen them. This whole mess has him more anxious than he already is.

I hope she is

"Doesn't it bother you that your wife is probably in the other room fucking her parkour instructor?" Vasco asks when Nik and him are finally alone.

Nik kisses him fully on the mouth before answering, "I hope she is."

Vasco pushes on, aware they are talking about feelings yet again. "I know you've been telling her to date that woman for years, but joking about it, and it actually happening... isn't it difficult?"

Nik kisses Vasco again, and Vasco almost forgets what they were talking about, but then Nik's lips are gone from his, and Nik is leaning back. Vasco fights the urge to follow.

"It was more difficult to deal with my own sexuality. Fuck, when I married Perce, I didn't even know I was bisexual—or pansexual or whatever. I had this dream when I was young: marry a pretty young woman, have a lot of kids, a few pets, and stay in love forever. My parents divorced when I was young, so I always wanted better. I wanted to be a better partner, a better parent, a better person. Just, you know, better."

Vasco pushes dreadlocks out of Nik's face. "A lot of that fantasy sounds like we could still do that. Except for me not having a uterus, of course."

Nik blushes again, and Vasco can't help but tease him for it. "For someone who swears up a storm on a good day, you are adorable when people talk about sex."

Nik takes a deep breath, and is clearly stealing himself for something. "When I had my first fantasies of sucking—" A very brief hesitation, before he pushes on. "—dick, I thought I was just weird."

Vasco laughs. "You are weird. But not because of that. Sorry, continue."

Nik pokes him in the chest. "Thanks? Anyway. Where was I?"

"Sucking dick," Vasco offers, and enjoys watching the color return to Nik's cheeks.

"Yeah, right. Isavella. When I dreamed of someone else fucking my wife, I thought I was a pervert. I thought I wanted to watch that."

"But you don't." It's not a question.

Nik laughs. "Fuck. Hell, no. I don't wanna see that."

"You know," Vasco admits, "I was thinking something similar earlier when Percy put her hand on yours."

Nik's eyes widen, and he starts his apology so fast Vasco has to interrupt it, even though he saw it coming. "No, no need for any of that. I was fine with it."

Nik looks unconvinced, so he kisses the man—okay, maybe it's also a tiny bit for himself—before he continues. "It wasn't about you and her. But I was surprised that I didn't care at all. Shouldn't I be jealous?"

Nik shrugs. "Should you? I've never been the best at emotional and social shoulda-woulda-coulda."

"Interesting way to phrase that. Huh." Vasco shakes his head to clear it. "Anyway, I saw her hand on yours, and I wasn't jealous. And that confused me a bit, because I would definitely not have been okay with Michael—my ex—doing that."

"What changed?"

It's Vasco's turn to shrug, though he thinks he knows the answer. "I trust you."

"Michael wasn't in any of the photos you showed me," Nik says after a moment. "Did you not want me to have to see them or do you not have any?"

Vasco leans his forehead against Nik's and closes his eyes. Nik's arm slides around him, comforting and strong. "Michael wasn't good for me. I only have one photo to remind me of that time. And he's not in it."

He snuggles into Nik, soaks up the warmth and closeness, but then pulls back to dig his phone out of his pocket. He scrolls through photos until he finds what he's looking for.

"You've seen it." He holds out his phone, the picture pulled up. "I just didn't tell you anything about the context."

It's a simple photo of a Hacienda-style vase. Upon closer inspection, thin lines web the surface where Ella and Josefine helped him glue the heirloom back together.

"I told you this was my grandmothers," he explains.

Nik returns the phone. "But there's more to the story."

Vasco nods. "He knew what the vase meant to me. When I didn't do what he wanted, he threatened to throw it. I didn't think he'd be that childish, so I didn't rise to the bait." He shudders. "Which was the end of that vase's ability to actually act as a vase." He points at the picture. "There's one piece missing near the bottom, you know?" He zooms in to show Nik, who just nods, clearly content to let him talk this off his chest. "It was also the end of our relationship, though that wake-up call had been way overdue if you believe Ella. Apparently, she knew all along that Michael was a gas-lighting drama queen and nothing but trouble."

But he hadn't. He'd made up excuse after excuse until his heart was in pieces, just like that stupid vase.

"You deserve to be treated so much better than that," Nik says with traces of anger in his voice.

"Can we go back to talking about your wife fucking the parkour instructor?" Vasco asks, desperate to stop thinking about just how much Michael hurt him.

"I have a better idea," Nik states, and opens a button on Vasco's shirt.

"I think I like that one better, too," Vasco agrees, and tries to speed up the unbuttoning process by opening buttons from the bottom. Nik, very gently, takes his hands in his, and pushes Vasco back into the mattress.

With an even gentler smile tugging on one corner of his mouth, Nik shakes his head. "My idea, my rules."

Vasco considers pointing out that he'll need to know the rules to obey them, but instead crosses his hands above his head, and submits.

Nik takes his time with every one of those way-too-many buttons, trailing kisses down the exposed skin after every one. By the time, he's taken Vasco's shirt off, Vasco is hard—and fighting almost as hard to keep his hands where they are.

He groans when Nik gets up, leaving cold air behind. Nik smiles, as he unceremoniously strips off his own shirt and undershirt with a lot less patience than he had for Vasco's clothes.

"I think I'm about to show you just how little I know about any of this," Nik admits, when he sits down on the edge of the bed, and opens a drawer on his nightstand. When his fingers emerge, he's holding a wrapped condom.

"I'd really like to fuck you," Nik admits, "and I've, um, done my research."

"But you've never done this before," Vasco finishes, as he pulls Nik closer. Nik doesn't resist, and lets himself get pulled back into bed.

"Can we forget that 'my rules' thing, because I'm fucking nervous right now, and I don't even know how to ask?" Nik's biting his bottom lip, a nervous tick Vasco can't help but kiss away.

"Guapo." He takes the condom from Nik, places it next to them on the bed, and looks into Nik's eyes. "There's no rush. We haven't done *that* yet, and if you aren't ready, you aren't ready."

Nik shakes his head. "No, no. That's not—I do. I want to. I need to. Fuck! I know why they don't teach this shit at school."

"They should," Vasco says, before he can stop himself.

Nik waves an impatient hand. "Yes, all that. Definitely. But, right now, I don't give a fuck, because—just look at yourself, man."

Vasco presses his hip into Nik's, and they both groan. Yeah, maybe not the time to talk about education.

"As I'm sure you have the general idea—" Nik nods, so he continues, "I am going to guess there's some part of this you are overthinking."

Nik laughs. "Definitely. Okay, fuck." He talks very, very fast, and Vasco almost doesn't catch the rest of the sentence. "Do you prefer fucking someone or getting fucked?"

"Top or bottom?" Vasco offers.

"That easy?"

Vasco chuckles. "Yeah. That easy."

Nik sighs. "In that case: top or bottom?"

"Bottom, so far, but I've never tried anything else, and am definitely open to some experimentation," Vasco says, talking almost as fast as Nik, because Nik has pressed himself into Vasco again, and he can barely keep his thoughts together long enough for this discussion that a girl and a boy would never have to get through—or figure out the vocabulary for.

Nik is grinning, and his words don't seem to match that expression. "I'm nervous," he admits, but when Vasco kisses him, Nik's hands slide around Vasco as if they've always belonged there.

Vasco lets Nik take him apart, piece by piece, teasing tremors out of him for what feels like hours, before he finally rips open that condom wrapper, and slides the condom on his dick to complete another first—a first for them, and a first for Nik.

Glad to be of service

"When I said I wanted to meet your parents, I didn't think it would be this soon," Nik says into the phone.

Vasco chuckles on the other end of the line. "Me neither, guapo. But it's time to loop them in. See you soon?"

Nik promises to be there, and hangs up the phone. He hasn't moved when there is a knock at his door, and Percy's voice comes from the other side. "Nik, do you want some dinner?"

He unfreezes, and stammers for Percy to come in. She opens the door and finds him in the middle of the room, still staring at his phone.

"Everything okay?" Percy asks, worried.

He pulls his gaze from the screen to look up at her. "Vasco's had an idea."

Percy takes him by the arm and leads them to their couch. "Tell me."

And Nik does. "I think Vasco just solved your biggest headache, Perce." She doesn't answer, doesn't interrupt, and Nik is acutely aware of how rarely he's had her undivided attention over the years. "That charity they run, Vasco thinks they'd be able to coordinate share distribution. I know you were worried about who would buy your shares once you let go of them." He takes a deep breath. "Well, their charity thing—I admit I still don't fully get what they do."

Percy hesitates, but seems to decide an interruption is worth it. "They help charities work together to unite efforts and to better distribute donations. It's kind of like a charity for charities."

Nik smiles. "That's some next-level good-doing."

"Actually, it's more like a non-profit coaching system for charities, but same difference." She sucks in a breath. "Damn it. I forgot." She jumps up. "Sorry, I know we're in the middle of something." She runs to the counter where she picks up her phone. "Sorry about that. Thank you so much for your patience."

She looks over at Nik, mouths, "Dinner?" and when he shakes his head, she orders for herself and hangs up the phone.

By the time her dinner arrives, he has explained Vasco's idea to her, and she has agreed to loop in his moms.

"I guess it's time for you to meet your boyfriend's parents," Percy says afterward, and Nik's chest flutters from nerves.

Nik rubs a hand over his hair. "I don't know if I should be more nervous about that or this idea of Vasco's."

She shoos him out of the door with a final "Good luck," and Nik drives to Vasco's house in auto-pilot mode.

He's half-way through an anxiety attack about whether he should ring the door bell or text Vasco, when the front door opens and Vasco steps out to greet him.

"Hola, guapo," he says, and grabs Nik's hand. Nik is vaguely aware that their fingers intertwine for a quick squeeze of comfort before Vasco grabs his entire hand instead.

Vasco pulls him through the front door. A welcoming warm light illuminates the hallway behind.

"Ready?" Vasco whispers, and Nik nods, though he doesn't think he'll ever be ready. "Ready as I'll ever be," he answers.

They step over the threshold, and Vasco calls for his family. Within seconds, half a dozen women show up from around corners, and Nik is sure they were waiting for them while trying to give them space.

"It's so nice to meet you," a blonde girl squeals before she hugs Nik tightly. "So nice!" She backs off a little, cheeks red. "Sorry, I'm a little too excited. Ella has told me so much about you."

Nik laughs. "Nice to meet you, too. Josephine, right?"

Josephine exchanges a knowing glance with Vasco. "The old race trick?" [4]

Nik can feel his cheeks flush, and stammers. "That obvious?"

Vasco grins, "Don't worry about it, Nik. No one expects you to remember all the names or keep everyone straight."

"Straight is hard to find in this house in general," Josephine dimples.

An Indian girl with thick brown curls who Nik guesses is Ella fakes a cough. "Speak for yourself, sis. Some of us haven't figured that out yet."

Jo waves her off. "Ah, just wait for it. You're gay as a clockwork orange."

Before they can continue their banter, Vasco interrupts. "Okay, Nik, let's get these introductions over with so we can sit down for dinner."

He indicates his sisters one after the other, and Nik gets hugged tightly by Ella, shakes the hands of Giaù and Dee, before Vasco introduces him to his parents.

"It's so nice to meet you, Nik," Anna Cohen says, as she shakes his hand. She waves him up and down, "Though I am not sure why Vasco here has kept you a secret for so long."

Her wife steps forward to take Nik's hand, and adds, "A not-so-well-kept secret, to be fair, but a secret nonetheless. It really is nice to finally meet the man whose been making our son grin like an idiot even more than usual."

"Mom!" Vasco complains, but he's grinning like a love-sick fool nonetheless.

Mama Cohen ushers them into the dining room where the plates are set for all of them, and a steaming pot stands in the middle of the table. A hearty smell hits Nik's nostrils the moment he enters the room. "That smells more than delicious."

While Susan ladles out the soup, Vasco leans closer to Nik. "You alright?"

Nik meets his eyes, and admits, "You've got a big family."

Vasco squeezes his knee under the table. "Let me know if you need a break."

"Ah, why would he need a break from us?" Josephine interjects. "Who wouldn't want to enjoy every second of a calming and quiet Cohen family dinner." She winks at Nik. "But, seriously. We know this is a lot, especially if you aren't used to it, so don't worry if you need to pretend to go to the bathroom more often than feels necessary."

"I see the non-judgement part runs in the family," Nik observes.

"Raised by the same two women," Dee answers, somehow aware of their conversation from the other end of the table. "Bread, Nik?"

Nik looks over to her and eyes the sliced baguette. He's about to wave it off with a thanks when Anna adds, "It's gluten-free. Don't worry. Vasco's made sure you can eat whatever we serve you."

"He's only been a bit anal about it," Dee explains, as he accepts the bread. "But, as we all know, it's quote-unquote better for you anyway, right?"

"Shouldn't it be 'quote word unquote,'" Nik says before he's wrapped his head around the words. "Fuck, I'm sorry." He slaps a hand over his mouth. "Sorry, sorry. I'm nervous."

Vasco grabs his hand, and places both their hands on Nik's leg. "Take a breath, Nik."

"Honestly," Ella says, "Don't worry so much. These two here—" She indicates their parents. "They are used to much worse. They've got me who can't stop swearing, Dee who can't stop correcting everyone in her path."

Gigi's quiet voice joins the mix. "It's actually quite ironic that you're giving her some of her own medicine."

"Right here, girls," Dee complains.

Ella bumps her shoulder into Dee's. "Ah, sis. But you know you are an insufferable know-it-all. It's part of your charm."

Conversation slows much to Nik's relief while they eat their soup. It's not until Anna carries the empty plates into the kitchen with helping hands from Ella and Josephine that Vasco's mom, Susan, addresses Nik again. "Vasco's told me not to address the elephant in the room until after dinner."

"Mom!" Vasco objects, but Susan pushes on. "So, I won't. Yet. Though I am more than curious. Instead, let's pretend this is a normal meet-the-boyfriend kind of dinner, okay?"

Nik fish-mouths a few time, then decides a nod will do, and stays silent.

"In that case: how about we start with the simplest questions: how old are you? Where did you grow up? What are you passionate about?"

"Apart from our dear brother, of course," Dee says.

Nik tries not to lose track of the questions, as he answers them one by one. "I'm two years younger than your son, 31. I grew up here in SoCal, a small town near San Diego to be precise. And—sorry, what was the third one again?"

Anna and her daughters return from the kitchen with three steaming pots, and Susan gets distracted for a few moments. She takes the heavy pot from her wife and sets it down in the middle of the table.

"What did we miss?" Anna asks and Gigi gives a succinct summary that proves she listens much more than she talks.

Anna sits down in her chair. "Oh, what town?"

"Oceanside, it's near—"

"Camp Pendleton," Anna finishes for him. "I was there as a consultant a few years ago. Oceanside, not the camp, I mean."

Nik, thrown off by being interrupted, takes a second to sort his thoughts. He feels Anna's eyes on him, and is grateful when Vasco stirs the conversation away from where he grew up. "And then Mom replaced the default job question with one about passion, I think."

"Jobs are so boring," Anna agrees with her wife. "Also, Ella told me you're a writer already."

More of a trophy husband who dabbles in journalism, Nik thinks but manages to keep the words in his head. Instead, he responds, "Which is also kind of an answer to the passion question." He holds his plate out to Susan who is dishing out their main course. "Thank you, Susan. I want to help humanity see that it's worth fighting for."

"Is it?" Dee asks, and she doesn't look like she's kidding.

Nik shrugs. "Yeah, I think so. Not all of us, of course. I'm the first to admit I'm not the biggest fan of most humans, but humanity as a whole kinda has me rooting for it."

Vasco rubs a hand over Nik's leg. "The same way you'd root for any species on the path to extinction."

Nik nods. "Yes, exactly. So, I write about social justice issues, environmental issues, and all those lovely things we humans keep fu—messing up."

"We fuck them up pretty nicely," Susan agrees with him, and even he knows she's swearing to make him feel better. He more than appreciates the gesture.

"You should've read his essay on gender-neutral language, mom," Vasco says. "It's right up your alley."

"You've gotta send me the link later," Susan request, and digs into her pasta. "This is delicious, honey," she adds after the first bite.

Anna smiles at her wife. "Thanks, of course, but this one is all Ella."

Susan pointedly turns to Ella. "This is delicious, honey."

Ella chuckles. "Thanks, mom."

As dinner progresses, Nik relaxes. And, very slowly, he begins to divide the sisters by their characteristics rather than their race.

"Did I tell you that I met Nik at the fundraiser?" Gigi asks after their main course has been cleared off the table.

Nik almost spits out his drink when he remembers what he said to Gigi that day. *Breasts can be so useful.*

He eyes Gigi warily, as she tells her parents all about how she helped him get a drink—thankfully without repeating his breast-related stupidity. No matter how open-minded the Cohens were, talking about the breasts of their underaged daughter surely wouldn't improve their opinion of him.

"It was so much fun to watch you fail," Ella laughs. "Vasco and I were having a blast."

Nik shrugs. "Glad to be of service."

Anna and Susan exchange a glance, and Nik knows they are running out of time before the elephant joins the conversation.

The elephant in the room

Nik's leg is bobbing up and down, and Vasco knows better than to try and stop it.

"No need to be nervous," he whispers, though he's sure at least Ella can hear them. He turns back to his parents and decides that it's time to move beyond small-talk. "Speaking of the fundraiser..."

Nik's faces loses some of it's color but his voice is steady when he says, "Time to address the elephant in the room?"

Vasco chuckles. "Something like that."

His mothers exchange a glance, then all eyes are on him and Nik. "So I'm allowed to ask why you're dating a married man now?" his mama asks and earns herself a reproaching look from his mom.

"I'm sure they'll get there," she says.

Vasco takes a sip from his cup before he starts to explain. He tells them about Bold Industries' plan to expand their drilling operations into the arctic. He tells them about Nik and Percy, about the board, about all of it.

"So, Percy will sell all of her shares before the next board election this January," he finishes. "But she's worried about who will buy them up when they are available."

No one speaks. Vasco quietly thinks it's probably the first time none of the women in his life can come up with anything to say.

"But Vasco thinks we might have a solution to this problem," Nik supplies. Nik's never good with silence, so Vasco isn't surprised he's the one to break it.

He indicates his mothers. "And that's where you all come in."

Anna grabs her wife's hand on the table. "I'm a bit speechless. Not least of all that you've managed to actually keep it all quiet."

Susan leans in. "So, what's the solution?"

Nik looks at Vasco, then says, "I've talked to Percy and if you can coordinate it, she'd like to donate her shares to charity. Not one charity, considering how many shares she holds. She'd prefer to spread it around a bit to get more minds into the decision-making processes."

"More minds at work, you mean," Vasco adds, and he can feel Nik's knee bob in the rhythm of "Work, work. I'm looking for a mind at work." Nik's referencitis might just be the cutest thing about him.

"Precisely," Nik answers when he's run through the catchy tune. "We're hoping others will follow suit. We've already had some people sell their shares, but I'm sure there will be a few more who held out because they thought Bold Industries might survive Percy stepping down." Nik sighs. "We'll be ruining a lot of lives. But we also hope to save a lot of them." He gestures toward Vasco's moms. "And with your help, we might actually be able to pull it off."

The silence that follows is absolute. Not even Josephine can think of anything to say to fill it. Nik takes a nervous sip of beer. Josephine refills her glass. After what feels like minutes, his mama turns to his mom, and Vasco knows there's a silent conversation that only they can follow. In the end, Susan nods, and they face Nik.

"Okay," Anna says. "Okay."

Susan leans forward. "But, if we're gonna do this, we want to be looped in all the way. We need to know what we are running into, so we can make sure we aren't screwing anyone over."

Her stare is fierce, and Vasco admires Nik for holding it. Nik who isn't good with eye-contact looks her full in the face and promises. "I can do that. I'll ask Percy to give you a call."

Susan's face softens, as she tells Vasco to pass on their personal numbers, though Vasco is sure Percy won't need them. If she managed to get a hold his number, he's sure she could get theirs.

With a very sudden return to family dinner, his mama gets up and declares it is time for desert. Before she leaves the room, she makes sure to ban any further conversation about work from the table.

"Told you they'd be in," he says quietly, and Nik smiles at him, the crooked smile Vasco wants to see so much more often.

"Thank you," Nik whispers back, before he turns to Gigi. "Hey, Gigi, you should've seen the face of that barkeeper when I told him to put the drinks on Percy's tab."

It takes Gigi a second, then she bursts out laughing. "Oh, I bet he was *very* nice to you after that."

"His boss's boss's boss or something, and he ignored me." Nik barks a laugh. "Yeah, he was more than nice."

When his parents return with three giant jars of ice cream, they pass them around and dig in. Nik and Jo exchange war stories that only people who are chronically ill seem to be able to laugh about, but their positivity is inspiring, and the mood only gets better as the evening ages.

When Ella and Jo excuse themselves, Vasco offers to help Jo upstairs. A quick glance at Nik to make sure he'll be alright, and he follows them into the hallway.

He can barely hear Gigi when she asks if she mentioned what Nik said to her when she got him drinks, followed by a defeated groan from Nik, and laughter, as he carries Josefine on his back up the stairs.

One day, Vasco will buy her a chair lift. Not that he minds carrying her.

She snuggles against his neck, and squeezes a bit tighter. "You found a good one, Vasco."

Ella squeezes his elbow. "I bet you can't wait for January anyway, right?"

Oh, how fucking right she is. He'd do almost anything to speed up time and declare Nik his. Nik's laughter is echoing through the house, and he wants more of it. He wants all of it.

I can do this

Nik is pacing. And there is nothing Vasco can do to help, because he can't even touch Nik right now. Instead, he watches, as Nik is walking grooves into the floor, as they wait for the evening to start.

"I don't think I can do this," Percy declares, and Isavella squeezes Vasco's arm more tightly.

"Of course you can," Nik says, his voice steady, though Vasco can see the panic behind his eyes. "We all can do this. I can do this."

It sounds like a mantra, one he's been repeating for hours. *I can do this. You can do this. We can do this. I can do this.*

And Vasco can fucking do this, too. He'll have to.

He follows Percy and Nik through a door and down a corridor. When Percy closes a door behind them, they are alone. Percy collapses onto a couch, and Isavella ditches Vasco for her without second thought.

Vasco walks over to where Nik has already started pacing again, and envelops the man in his arms. "I'm here, guapo. I'm here."

Nik's breaths are fast and shallow, and Vasco can feel the meltdown coming. But Nik can't break down right now.

"Nik, look at me." He grabs Nik's face in his hands. "Guapo, look at me."

Nik lets his chin be dragged upward, meets Vasco's gaze. "I'm here, babe."

Another mantra. And he's gonna follow it with Nik's. "You can do this. We all can."

The corner of Nik's mouth twitches. "That's my line."

Vasco chuckles. "Can you patent a statement like that?"

He knows he's prevented the impeding meltdown when Nik's face grows stern. "If Driscoll's can have a trademark on 'Only the finest berries,' I should be allowed to. You should see the things people have patents, copyrights, and trademarks on."

He decides to push Nik toward the rant rather than preventing it. Better a rant than a meltdown. Distraction will be good for Nik. "Yeah, like what?"

He's vaguely aware of Isavella's attempts to calm Percy, but she seems to got this, so he focuses on Nik.

"There's a fucking copyright on the Eiffel Tour." Nik shakes his head. "Well, on the lights. The tower is public domain, as far as I know, but those lights? They are art—and copyrighted."

Vasco thinks of the millions of postcards of the Eiffel Tour, and suddenly wonders if they all had to pay licensing fees, but he doesn't get to follow the thought, because Nik isn't done.

"Some colors, too." Nik sits on a stool. "Oh, and Dark Vader's breathing from the movies."

Vasco stares. "You can get a trademark on breathing? Shouldn't that be illegal."

Nik looks ready for a rant-detour into things that should be considered common goods but aren't but Percy's phone rings, and they all jump.

Nik looks ready to vomit, so Vasco pulls him into this arms one final time, whispers all their mantras yet again, before they are off toward the stage.

Halfway there, Percy starts whispering urgently, and Isavella pulls her into another room. "We'll be right there."

They leave them to meet his family outside where a crowd has started to gather. Ushers are checking invitations and bags. A lot hinges on tonight.

And then the doors are closing, and all their guests are seating around tables in the ballroom. Vasco looks around and the feeling of deja-vu is stronger than ever.

They are back at the mansion where he first saw Nik, told him about Ursa major, and shared a joint.

Isavella takes the seat next to him, and he grabs her hand. Their fingers intertwine, and they sit in silence, as Percy leads Nik up the stairs. Ella leans over, takes his other hand.

Showtime.

I am done standing by+++

Nik feels set back in time surrounded by the same boring suits that attended the pre-holiday gala. But this time, he's up on stage with Percy, and they are in this together. He follows her onto the stage, and stands next to her at the podium.

She squeezes his hands, and he notices he's not bothered by it. She didn't slide her fingers into his. Ironic that it took their separation to make her learn how to hold his hand.

He hadn't been the only one who'd half-assed their marriage.

She smiles at the assembled suits and dresses, and tabs the screen of the podium to pull up her speech.

"My dear guests, thank you so much for coming. Welcome to Bold Industrie's annual shareholder gala." She slightly adjust the microphone. "When I last stood on a stage, I declared I'd sell my shares. I admit, that I was afraid of this step. It wasn't the financial outlook that scared me most, though. I was scared I would be giving up my legacy in vain."

Nik finds Vasco, his family, and Isavella on a table in the front. Vasco is smiling up at him, and Nik can't wait to get this over with.

"No one could assure me that my shares would not merely be bought up by greedy hands with large wallets. I was scared.

But thanks to my husband and two wonderful women, I am not scared anymore. Today, I am donating every single one of my shares to charities all over the world."

A collective gasp runs through the gathered guests, but Percy keeps talking, and the chatter quickly dies down, as no one seems to want to miss a word of her speech.

"When my father addressed you in September, he was joined by Susan and Anna Cohen, who are here again tonight. Over the last weeks, they have worked tirelessly with me to ensure that my legacy won't be going to waste—and to help humanity toward a better future."

A few people clap, but most are still to spellbound to react.

"In January, when the new board is elected, every share will matter, so I have given up every single one of mine. And today—" She looks around the room with a fire in her eyes that Nik hasn't seen in years. "—I urge you to follow suit.

"When my father addressed you, he talked a big talk about saving the environment and social justice by raising funds for the Cohens. And I stood idly by and let him lie to all of your faces. You can't donate to charity on the one side while planning to expand drilling into a fragile ecosystem like the Arctic."

She sighs deeply. "I stood by and let him, but I am done standing by. My husband, Nik," she continues with a glance at him, "has been working toward a better future for this planet, for humanity, for years, but I wasn't able to see it."

Vasco's smile anchors Nik, as he listens to his wife and checks the crowd's reactions.

"I wasn't able to see how much of a bubble I lived in. I was comfortable. But I was unhappy."

Percy clears her throat. She takes a sip of water, slowly returns the glass to the podium, and lets go of Nik's hand. A cold chill remains behind when her warmth leaves.

"Humanity is living in a bubble. And we need to burst it before it is too late. Too many people are in charge who care more about their bottom line than the future–or even present life. In many ways, capitalism is like religion. It only works if we believe in it. And I'm not sure I'm still a believer."

She steps around the podium and walks toward the edge of the stage. Nik stays, as foreboding tingles on his scalp.

"For the past weeks—" she continues, and Nik knows she's gone off-script—at least the script he wrote for her. "—I've had to do a lot of pretending to keep things from falling apart. And I've long considered if I should keep pretending for one more night."

She walks to the very edge of the stage. "Instead, I want to tell you about a man I met a few weeks ago. A man who bought shares for the wrong reasons and returned them for the right ones."

Nik suppressed a smile, as he remembered the encounter. In his opinion, the man had returned them for the wrong reasons, too, but maybe Percy's generosity would stick in his head next time. Maybe.

"Tonight, I am talking to those of you who bought shares for the wrong reasons, those of you who told themselves they'd do good with the profit they made, those of you who lied to themselves." Nik recognized those words. He'd written them. Not completely off-script after all.

"Well, if I am right about you, you deserve my honesty." She walks toward the stairs at the side of the stage. "I've had to do a lot of pretending. For weeks, I've pretended to be a wife to spare some, let's say, traditional men from opening their minds." She takes a step down."I've pretended to be a good wife for them. And I've asked others to pretend with me."

Two more steps down the stairs. "But you deserve my honesty."

She reaches the bottom of the stairs and crosses the empty space between the stage and the table with Isavella and Vasco. When she reaches them, she holds out a hand for Isavella. Nik can't make out her expression, but watches as she gets up and follows Percy up the stairs to the stage, her bottle-green ballgown swirling around her ballerinas.

"I've been married to Nikau for more than a decade." She looks around at him and smiles, but he's too frozen to react. And so, it seems, is the audience. The crowd seems to be holding their breath. "We were never right for another, but one thing led to another, and it wasn't until my husband met a wonderful man outside this very building that we both realized it was time to get a divorce." She takes a deep breath. "That day, my father passed away and left me this company." She takes Nik's hand, the three of them joined on stage. "I married a good man, one of the best. And Nik stayed. I've asked a lot of him over these last few weeks. At first, we wanted to stop the Arctic project, but even that seemed like an uphill battle, and I knew many wouldn't accept me as their superior as a woman."

Nik stares at Vasco and tries to breathe.

"So, we kept pretending and dated the people who were right for us in secret." She pulls Isavella closer. "There will be a new board in January, and I trust you with my truth because I believe in you. I believe in us. I believe we can do this."

A whoop from the back of the room breaks the silence and Nik recognizes the man with the yellow-duck-tie. A few people join in, some clap. Most stare. And then all hell breaks loose as people start chattering.

Percy clears her throat. "I know, it's a lot. If I could ask for another minute of your time, please." She waits a moment, tries again. "Please, I want to address some of the many questions you are sure to have."

After another moment, the room begins to quiet, and Percy finishes her speech.

"We know that donating the shares will cause many to flee what they think is a sinking ship, but I assure you we will take care of every single one of you. Things won't happen overnight. This will be an uphill battle. But we can do this. All of us together. So, again, I urge you—" She takes a moment to meet the eyes of the crowd. "Follow my lead and donate your shares. If you don't know how or need any help whatsoever, please talk to the Cohen Foundation for guidance. We are all in this together."

And with that, she taps the button on her mic and drags both of them off-stage. She lets go of Nik's hand and embraces Isavella before they face the already forming sea of people with questions. But there is only one person Nik wants to see right now, so he walks over to Vasco who is on his feet before Nik reaches him, take the man's hand, and walks toward the door.

It's chilly outside, but there is a nice bench just off the premises where they can watch the stars.

Everywhere?

Marvin shakes the water out of his fur. Despite the shouted warning ahead, Vasco gets a full blast. He laughs, as he wipes the water from his face. "Thanks, Marv, very refreshing."

Marvin puts her paws on his chest and licks the droplets of his face, and Nik can't stop laughing as Vasco sputters.

Marvin runs back into the water, chasing waves. Nik pulls Vasco closer, sliding an arm around the man's hip, and kisses him.

"I wanted to get you a record player for your birthday," he says after a while, as they continue their walk along the beach, the waves playing around their bare feet. "But I didn't know if you'd be able to take it."

Vasco looks around at him, confusion clear enough on his face for even Nik to understand. "Take it where?"

Nik's mouth pulls up. "Everywhere?"

Vasco raises an eyebrow. "Everywhere?"

Nik strokes Vasco's cheek, takes a breath, and says, "You know how you always said you'd like to learn more about where you came from, your heritage?"

Vasco nods, but his expression is still mostly confused.

"I've talked to your parents. Ella has been helping me fig—"

Vasco laughs. "I knew she was keeping a secret!"

"Yes, babe, she was. Mine." He kisses Vasco, but they break apart quickly, Vasco clearly too curious about Nik's news. "I really hope you, ah, nevermind. Here we go." He drives his hands through his hair before returning them to Vasco's back. "Ella and I have planned a route for us. It won't be all vacation, but we'll be able to explore. Fuck, I'm not making any sense, am I?"

"Not really, wanna try again?" Vasco pulls him onto the sand, and they sit facing the waves where Marvin is still fighting his never-ending battle against the attacking waves and having the time of his life.

"Your parents agreed to give me a job," Nik tries again. "Us, actually. We'll be visiting their charity partners all over the globe." He holds up airquotes. "'To strengthen the relationships' or whatever your mom called it."

Vasco leans back on his elbows. "What jobs?"

Nik smiles, "I'll be starting a column for them, interviewing their partners, telling the stories of locals, of projects that worked, failures along the way."

Vasco sits up abruptly. "Nik, that's amazing. Isn't that exactly what you wanted to do?"

Nik's smile is soft. "Yes, it is. I never thought..." He trails off, his gaze on the horizon.

Vasco puts an arm around him, kisses his cheek. "Tell me more."

"If you agree, we'll start in New Zealand. Ella helped me plan the route."

Vasco grins, "Isn't that your heritage more than mine?"

Nik smiles, "I wanted to start in Mexico, but Ella convinced me it made more sense to start in New Zealand spring and get out of there before winter."

Vasco's knowing look tells Nik he doesn't need to explain about seasons and the Southern hemisphere. "Well, we'll be meeting some charities there who work on marine protection. Then, we'll take a boat to Tasmania, travel up the coast to the Great Barrier Reef."

Nik's chest flutters. He knows it will be months before they can leave. He knows Vasco has to finish his degree. But it's a dream, a plan, their future. Well, if Vasco agrees, that is.

"Ella has an entire route planned out for us. She's spent a lot of time on it. Did you know she's a wizard with organization?"

Vasco's face is split in a wide grin. "She's a natural planner, that one."

"Anyway, we'll get to see a lot. It won't be a vacation—"

Vasco kisses Nik before he can say anything else. Nik digs his hands into Vasco's hair, and lets himself sink into the kiss.

"I'm in," Vasco says after a while, and Nik can't believe this is his life.

"So, better than a record player?"

Another kiss is all the answer Nik gets, but it says more than a thousand words.

---

[1] Reference: Red, White, and Royal Blue by Casey McQuiston

[2] Protecting the global ocean for biodiversity, food and climate by Sala et al (2021)

[3] Massively multiplayer online role-playing game

[4] If you get as confused by all the women in this scene as Nik, refer to the list of characters at the beginning of the book.

Don't miss out!

Visit the website below and you can sign up to receive emails whenever Kate Breuer publishes a new book. There's no charge and no obligation.

https://books2read.com/r/B-A-EJZR-ZWNAF

Connecting independent readers to independent writers.

Did you love *With Feeling Plus Stuff*? Then you should read *Spores*[1] by Kate Breuer!

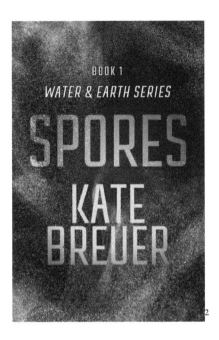

When the surface of the earth becomes uninhabitable, humans flee underneath the oceans. Well, those who are lucky enough to get into the utopia. Many are left fighting for limited living space in cave systems created by the last large earthquake in the San Andreas Fault. Those who didn't get into the bubble cities live alongside those who didn't uphold the high standards of the society.

Read more at https://katehildenbrand.com/.

---

1. https://books2read.com/u/4NyOyJ
2. https://books2read.com/u/4NyOyJ

Also by Kate Breuer

Water & Earth
Spores

Standalone
Out of Hiding
Chase: The Trilogy
With Feeling Plus Stuff

Watch for more at https://katehildenbrand.com/.

About the Author

Kate has been reading and writing for as long as she can remember. As a child she could be found cooped up in armchairs, snuggled in beds, or propped inside door frames reading books like *The Little Prince* and *The Diary of a Young Girl* despite being a bit younger than its target audience.

During a summer vacation at her grandmother's house, she wrote her first story about a cigarette going on an adventure to avoid death by fire. This morbidly fun tale was inspired by her grandmother's chain-smoking habits.

Reading a poem at her best friend's funeral as a teenager made her realize just how much power words hold.

With the help of Moony, Wormtail, Padfoot, and Prongs, as well as Bilbo, Frodo, Pippin, and the like, she wrote fantasy novels and short stories. One of her first finished books and possibly the most embarrassing part of her writing career was a sequel to Tolkien's The Lord of the Rings.

It was years before she moved on to original work and even longer before any of it had much value. In 2015, she wrote her first published novel during *NaNoWriMo*--well, a very rough first draft. After a long four years, it was finally edited, and more books always in her mind.

Keep dreaming, but also, please, keep thinking.

Read more at https://katehildenbrand.com/.